Palestine

DW Duke

PublishAmerica
Baltimore

First printing

All characters in this book are fictitious, and any resemblance to real persons, living or dead, is coincidental.

PublishAmerica has allowed this work to remain exactly as the author intended, verbatim, without editorial input.

ISBN: 978-1-4489-4611-2
PUBLISHED BY PUBLISHAMERICA, LLLP
www.publishamerica.com
Baltimore

Printed in the United States of America

I

As Katsín Akademái Bakhír (Senor Academic Officer) Aaron Levy drove the Humvee into the sandy ravine he heard the repeating sound of machine gun fire and the metallic ring of shots strafing the side of the vehicle he was driving. Suddenly, he heard a thunderous blast as the Humvee jolted up and rightward responding to the impact of a launched grenade. As the vehicle flew through the air, in what seemed like an eternity, Aaron looked to his right side to see the body of Rav Samál Rishón (First Seargent) Jacobson thrown forward, his skull shattering against the windshield. "Michael" Aaron shouted as blackness became his own limited awareness. Lapsing in and out of consciousness he crawled through the window of the overturned Humvee pulling his M4A1 assault rifle after him. Looking into the rear compartment he noted the lifeless body of Simon the nineteen year old from Tel Aviv, his body riddled with bullet wounds. The wheels of the Humvee continued to spin as he heard the familiar sound of angry Palestinian voices shouting something in Arabic concluding each utterance with "A'lah." Instinctively, Aaron lifted the M4A1 above the bottom of the overturned Humvee and fired a round in the direction of the voices. He raised his head in time to see three Palestinian soldiers fall to the ground then he heard only silence.

After waiting a few moments to assure that there were no others with the attackers, Aaron began to examine the injured soldiers under his command. With a sense of responsibility and anguish he asked, "What's your status, David?"

David looked at Aaron with a distressed expression as he said, "I'm hit in the leg."

"You're going to make it," replied Aaron. "Hold on."

"Jonathan, are you hit?" Aaron asked.

"I'm good, but Simon and Michael didn't make it," replied Jonathan.

Grabbing the broken radio with his right hand to report his position, Aaron felt a cold shiver as he found the communication device inoperative. Reaching to his belt for his cellular telephone he felt a sense of relief as he heard the device power on only to find that he could not obtain a signal. "Do either of you have your cell phones?" he asked.

"I didn't bring mine," replied David.

"I don't have one," said Jonathan, as he began to look for one on the belt of Simon. "I can't find one on Simon," he said.

"Michael doesn't seem to have one either," said Aaron. "I am going to look over the hill to get our bearings. Jonathan you collect the weapons and supplies. We are several miles inside the Strip (Gaza). It may take us some time to get out of here. We are going to have to move at night so bring the night vision goggles. I will be back in a few minutes. If any more Palestinians show up, fight like you have never fought before. We don't want to be taken alive."

As Aaron stood to his feet he felt a sharp sheering pain in his left leg. Looking down he discovered a gapping wound at mid femur. He could not tell if it was from a bullet entry or a result of the crash of the Humvee and he did not recall feeling any pain in his leg earlier. As he ran with a weak limp toward the top of the hill, Aaron suddenly heard more shouting voices behind him. He cleared the top of the hill and dove to the other side. Lying prostrate Aaron looked back over the hill to see a dozen Palestinian soldiers run up to the overturned Humvee. His immediate reaction was to open fire then he realized that his gun was empty. He did not have time to reload. He watched in horror as the Palestinians began jumping up and down, shouting and firing multiple rounds into the Humvee and into his comrades who had not even attempted to return fire. "They must have thought they would be taken prisoner," thought Aaron. In shock at what he had just witnessed, Aaron could do nothing but lie prostrate in the sand daring not to move a muscle. As he watched, the image of the Palestinians shouting and firing guns into the Humvee reminded him of a time long ago which set him on the course of his military life in the Israeli Defense Forces.

Long Ago

It was 1983. Five year old Aaron Levy was riding in the rear seat of the rented Volvo. His father was driving and his mother was sitting in the front passenger side of the vehicle cradling Aaron's infant sister Rebecca in her arms. Aaron's two year old sister Sarah sat in the rear seat next to Aaron. "I am so glad we made this trip," said Aaron's father, Dr. David Levy, with a kindly smile and a wink at Aaron in the rear view mirror. "This is our true homeland. Just think, our ancestors walked along this road toward Jerusalem three thousand years ago. It is definitely a different place from our home in San Diego." As they drove down the barren road toward Jerusalem, the family joked and marveled at the historic atmosphere. "It is definitely the land of HaShem," said Aaron's mother. "Someday, maybe we will make our aliyah."

"What is aliyah," asked Aaron.

"Aliyah is the call of every Jew to come home to Israel," said Aaron's father. "It says in the Zohar that every night the soul of a Jew goes to be with HaShem when he sleeps. The presence of HaShem is so awesome and wonderful that the soul does not want to return to earth. That is the reason it is so hard to wake up in the morning. But HaShem knows what is best so he sends the soul back to earth to live another day until finally one day, HaShem says, you may stay with me now. Then the person does not awaken. The desire to remain with HaShem is like aliyah which is the unexplainable desire of every Jew to be in Israel."

"What causes dreams," asked Aaron.

"Dreams are very interesting," said Dr. Levy. "As a neurologist I can tell you from a medical perspective what occurs in the brain when one dreams. But the sages tell us spiritually what happens. Dreams are the communication from the spiritual world. Often important information comes to us in dreams. Jacob's dream was a turning point in his life. Sometimes we have bad dreams when the soul is in conflict. Sometimes the bad dreams forewarn of impending danger. Sometimes they reflect a conflict within the relationship between HaShem and the recipient of the dream."

"I had a bad dream last week," said Aaron.

"What was it," asked Aaron's mother.

"I dreamed that we were in a car and people were trying to hurt us," said Aaron. "It was really scary."

Suddenly Aaron's mother shouted, "Look out," as a man dressed in black with a black hood over his head ran out in front of the car. Aaron's father swerved to avoid hitting the hooded assailant. As the Volvo veered off the road and crashed into a boulder several more men in black hoods ran out from behind a rock and began firing guns into the car. Aaron saw his father slump over the wheel as the blasting sound of the guns rang in his ears. He looked at Sarah next to him and could see the look of terror on her face. Aaron looked up through the open window to see a hooded terrorist looking in at him. Suddenly, the hooded assailant pointed the gun at two year old Sarah and fired one shot into her head and one into her body. He then stepped back and shot Aaron's mother point blank in the face as she tried to shield Rebecca with her own body. The assailant then pulled his mother's body off of Rebecca as a second assailant fired two shots into the body of the infant. The first assailant then pulled off his hood, looked at Aaron and began laughing. He pointed his pistol at Aaron's face and pulled the trigger but the gun was out of ammunition. Suddenly, Aaron heard shots in the distance as an IDF vehicle approached at a high rate of speed. The assailants jumped into a beat up pickup truck and sped away with the IDF soldiers in pursuit.

Aaron stared at the bodies of his mother, father and two sisters as the IDF officers attempted in vain to revive them. One of them took him by the shoulder and said something in Hebrew Aaron did not understand. The officer then asked, "Atah meveen Ivreet?"

Aaron replied, "Lo, ani Americai."

"Let's go over here," said the soldier in English as he led Aaron away from the scene of the crime. "My name is David, What is your name?"

Aaron replied, "Aaron Levy."

"Where are you from?" asked the officer.

"San Diego, California," replied Aaron.

"Is this your family?" asked David.

"Yes," said Aaron.

"Are you on vacation?" asked the soldier.

"Yes," replied Aaron. "We are on vacation."

David tried to distract Aaron who stood at the side of the rode watching the bodies of the members of his family as they were placed one by one into the back of the military vehicles. The events of that day seared into the brain of Aaron like hot burning coals. The tragedy of terrorism, and the loss of his family, left an impact upon his life that he would never forget. The IDF soldiers who appeared in the face of death and saved Aaron's life left a feeling of gratitude mixed with sorrow. Aaron knew then that he would someday make his aliyah to Israel just as his mother had said, and then he would become an IDF soldier.

II

Aaron Levy stood in front of his first year anatomy classroom at Washington University School of Medicine in St. Louis, Missouri. He was a member of the entering class of 2001. After returning from his trip to Israel where he lost his family, Aaron went to live with his uncle Samuel Levy a prominent medical malpractice defense attorney in St. Louis. He often visited Barnes Jewish Hospital with his uncle who would interview professors retained to serve as expert witnesses in cases he defended. His father had graduated from Washington University and it was Aaron's dream to attend Washington University School of Medicine like his father. The day of his acceptance was the day that Aaron thought his life had begun again.

As he waited to get into his classroom Aaron noticed a young woman on the opposite side of the hall who seemed to be looking at him. Aaron was amazed at her striking beauty. Her skin was slightly dark and her hair and eyes were jet black. "She looks like she might be Arab," thought Aaron. Suddenly, Aaron was startled as he noticed that she was walking toward him. "Excuse me," she said with a strong Middle Eastern accent. "Are you taking anatomy and physiology?"

"Yes," replied Aaron.

"Were you able to get your books," she asked. "The bookstore was out. I couldn't do my reading assignment. My anatomy class just got out. Fortunately, the professor didn't call on me."

"You can borrow mine if they don't have them later today," replied Aaron. "I will study something else while you use mine then I will study anatomy while you study something else."

"Oh thank you so much," she said. "You are a life saver."

"Where are you from," asked Aaron.

"I am from Palestine," she replied. Her words sent a chill down Aaron's spine as he remembered the vivid day he lost his family. He felt as though a door slammed in his path. He became flustered and lost the color in his face. "You are Jewish," she said. "I noticed your yarmulke."

"Yes, I am," replied Aaron.

"I have many Jewish friends in Palestine and Israel," she said. "My father works at a hospital in Israel and he travels across the border every day. Sometimes when I was a child he would take me with him. That is when I decided to become a doctor." She paused and looked at Aaron. "Are you okay? You suddenly got quiet," she asked. "I hope I didn't say something offensive."

"No, of course not," Aaron said. "You didn't say anything wrong." Aaron shuffled nervously as he tried to devise a way to get out of his commitment to allow her to use his anatomy book. "Your people killed my family," he thought.

"What is your name," she asked.

"My name is Aaron," he replied. "What is your name?"

"My name is Al Zahra," she said. "May I have your phone number so I can call you if they don't have any books later today?"

Aaron felt trapped. "Yes," he said not knowing how to get out of his commitment. He wrote the phone number of his aunt and uncle's residence and gave it to her.

"Thank you so much," she said. "I will try to not bother you unless I have to. I know you are busy."

"Don't worry about it," Aaron replied. "You have to study." Aaron thought, "What am I going to do if she calls. Uncle Simon or Aunt Sarah will recognize the Middle Eastern accent and they will ask questions. They will think she is my girlfriend and if she is not Jewish, in our orthodox family that will not be well received."

"Alright then," Al Zahra said. "I have to go to my next class. I will see you around."

"Ok," he replied.

That night at approximately 7:00 pm Aaron sat at the desk in his uncle's den as he studied anatomy. "This is much harder than undergraduate anatomy classes," he thought. Suddenly the phone rang. "I got it," Aaron shouted hoping to answer first just in case it was Al Zahra. "Hello," Aaron said.

"May I speak with Aaron," said the female voice on the other end with a strong Middle Eastern accent.

"This is Aaron," he replied. "Is this Al Zahra?"

"Yes it is," she replied. "How did you know?"

"Your accent is very distinct," he replied.

"Oh. I went by the bookstore today and they still don't have any anatomy books. I was hoping that maybe I could take you up on your earlier offer."

"Oh sure," said Aaron nervously. "Where do you want to meet?"

"I don't want to make you drive since I am the one borrowing the book. Where do you live?"

"We can't really study at my house," replied Aaron fabricating a white lie. "It gets too noisy around here. I live by the Central campus on Forsyth in Clayton. Do you know where the law school is located?"

"Yes," she replied.

"I will meet you in the front entrance to the law school. We can study there."

"Okay," she said. "I will see you in about oh, 30 minutes."

"That's perfect," Aaron replied. As he hung up the phone Aaron felt a tinge of excitement. "What am I doing," he thought. "This is crazy. She is probably Muslim."

"I am going out for a little while," Aaron told his aunt. "Don't wait up for me."

"Ok, be careful," Aunt Sarah replied.

Aaron watched Al Zahra walk up the sidewalk as he waited by the entrance to the law school. "She is so beautiful," he thought.

"Hi Aaron," Al Zahra said as she entered the building. "Thank you so much for helping me. You have saved my life. I do have some bad news though. According to the clerk at the bookstore, they won't have any more books for at least two to three weeks. The publisher is back ordered. I guess everyone wants to go to medical school," she laughed.

"That's okay, I don't mind sharing," Aaron said nervously.

As they sat on a couch in the hall of the law school they talked about simple matters. "When did you come to America?" asked Aaron.

"I came for my undergraduate work. I got my bachelors at UCLA. Where did you do your undergraduate work?" she asked.

"I did my undergraduate studies here at Washington University," he replied. Aaron shuffled as he fostered the courage to ask the ultimate question. "You said that your father worked at a hospital in Israel but you lived in Palestine. Do you mind if I ask a personal question?"

"Of course not," she replied. "What do you want to know?"

"What is your religion?" Deep inside Aaron was praying that she would say that she is Jewish.

"I am Muslim," she replied.

"Oh," Aaron said with a forced smile as his heart sank. "I could have fallen for this girl," he thought as he looked into her beautiful black eyes. "But now it can never be."

"Does it bother you that I am Muslim," she asked.

"Oh, of course, not," replied Aaron. "I mean, it isn't like we are romantically involved or anything." Aaron's face flushed with a little embarrassment.

"Oh no, of course not," laughed Al Zahra. "I mean, we haven't done or said anything to each other that would suggest that we are ever going to be romantically involved." She paused for a moment then asked, "We aren't going to be are we?"

Aaron suddenly reached for his soda out of nervousness and spilled it on the floor. "We can't," he said. "Your religion doesn't allow it and my religion doesn't allow it. How could we ever be romantically involved?"

"Oh no," Al Zahra whispered barley audibly as she threw her head back and looked at the ceiling. She paused for a moment then said, "You are right. Ours is not to be romantic. You are just being kind to me by sharing your book and I will be eternally grateful. It's getting late. I suppose we better say goodnight."

"Yes, you are right. Let's say goodnight. Let me walk you to your car. It isn't safe for a woman on campus at night," said Aaron.

"Oh, thank you," she replied. As they walked they talked of unimportant matters and said goodnight again.

Every evening for several weeks Aaron and Al Zahra would meet to study together and to share the anatomy book. Sometimes they would meet at the medical school and sometimes at a local restaurant. On some occasions, they would study early in the morning before classes as well and sometimes they would even meet in between classes. One evening as they were walking to Al Zahra's car, she said, "Aaron, can I be painfully candid?"

"Sure," he replied.

"You know my whole life I have known what I want to find in a man. I know this from the perspective of physical appearance, personality and intelligence. I already enjoy our sweet forbidden friendship. I can tell you that in just the short time I have known you, that you are everything that I have ever wanted in a man. You are him. You are the man I have always dreamed of finding. When I saw you in the hall the day we met, just from your appearance my heart jumped. It was like A'lah gave me a gift. There is just one problem. When I was talking to you and you looked to the side I saw your yarmulke. I know we can never be together because you are a Jew and I am a Muslim. Wouldn't you figure that would happen. I am being forward because I know that it can never be. But I just want to thank you for being so kind to me."

Aaron was speechless. He couldn't decide what to say to Al Zahra. As she noticed his uncertainty, Al Zahra said, "You don't have to say anything Aaron. I have never been this forward before. I don't know what got into me. My family would be shocked if they heard what I just said." They both laughed. Then she said, "I will see you tomorrow Aaron," as she leaned forward and gave Aaron his first kiss.

After they said goodnight Aaron's heart leaped. "What am I feeling," he thought. "Why am I feeling this excitement? Is this wrong? It will be a wonderful sweet friendship. How can such wonderful feelings be wrong? After all, didn't HaShem place these emotions in my heart? Didn't he bring us together for this sweet friendship?"

It was in the early morning September 11, 2001. Aaron and Al Zahra had decided to meet for breakfast at a small kosher café on Forest Park Ave. When Aaron arrived at the café Al Zahra was already sitting at an outside table. As he walked up to her he could see that she had been crying.

"What's wrong?" asked Aaron as she looked up at him.

Al Zahra stood to her feet and ran toward Aaron then gave him a hug. "You haven't heard the news have you?"

"No," replied Aaron. "I just took a shower then I came straight here." Aaron looked around and noticed that everyone seemed to be in shock. They were all watching the television in the cafe. As he looked at the screen Aaron noticed that there was a picture of two burning buildings. "What is that," he asked.

"Aaron, somebody flew two airplanes into both towers of the World Trade Center. One plane flew into each of the buildings. The authorities suspect terrorists. The buildings have collapsed and thousands of people are dead. They don't know the exact count yet but some are estimating in excess of 6000 people."

Aaron slowly sat down at the table. The vivid memory of his parents being killed by the murderers in Israel came to his thoughts. He looked at Al Zahra with a blank expression.

"Aaron, are you ok?" she asked.

"I just can't believe this is happening," he replied. "Why would anyone do something so crazy? The people flying the planes had to die too," he said.

"I just pray that they weren't Muslim," she said. "The extremists in our faith cause so much destruction and they cause the world to believe that we are all violent. According to my father, the Koran forbids terrorism."

Aaron replied with a puzzled expression on his face, "Your father says that?"

"Yes," she replied, as she nervously pulled out her copy of the Qur'an feeling necessity to prove her point. "Right here," she said frantically pointing to some verses in the second sura (chapter).

"You know Al Zahra, many people believe that Islam is a violent religion that advocates genocide for non-believers." said Aaron.

"That just isn't true," she replied. "Aaron, what do you believe about Muslims? Do you believe we are pagan? Do you believe we are violent and do you believe that we should not be allowed to live in Israel?"

Aaron paused momentarily then he said, "I believe that HaShem gave Israel to the Jews but that does not mean that non-Jews are prohibited from living there. The Jews were to set up a system of government that was fair to everyone. Instead, what happened is that some of the Zionists believed that they had to run everyone out of Israel who was not a Jew. We are told in the Torah at Shemot (Exodus) 23:9: That Jews are not to oppress the non-Jew in Israel. We have clear admonitions in the Talmud telling us that Jews were not to take a stronghold in Israel until the arrival of Moshiach ben David. 'Gerei toshav' is a term that refers to non-Jews who do not worship idols. According to the 10th Chapter of the Laws of Kings, provided they observe the seven laws of 'Bnei Noach,' with an understanding that those laws come from the Torah, they may live in Israel and even own land. In essence they are to be treated as Jews. When the Zionists first came to Israel, the Arabs wanted to form a single unified government, but the Zionists refused. The Arabs claim that they were driven from Israel but the Zionists say they left of their own free will. Either way they were not supposed to leave. According to Rambam, one of the great teachers of Judaism, a noahide is to be permitted to live in Israel as long as he follows the seven noahide laws. If they follow those laws they are to have all the rights of Jews. The seven noahide laws were the laws that were given to man before the law was given to the Israelites by Moses. If a gentile follows all of these seven laws, he is considered a righteous gentile and according to the Talmud he is as righteous as the greatest Jewish sage."

"What are the seven noachide laws," she asked.

"These are the seven noachide laws," said Aaron.

"Avodah Zarah: Do not worship false gods.

Shefichat damim: Do not commit murder.

Gezel: Do not steal.

Gilui arayot: Do not participate in sexual exploitation.

Birkat HaShem: Do not blaspheme HaShem (G-d).

Ever min ha-chai: Do not be cruel to any living thing including animals.

Dinim: Set up a system of government and courts of law to enforce the other six laws."

"Do you believe that Muslims who follow all of these seven laws should be permitted to live in Israel with all the rights of a Jew even now before Moshiach comes?" she asked.

"Yes," said Aaron. "They must keep all seven laws and recognize that those laws came from HaShem and were given in the Torah. Some interpret Rambam to say that if they design any system of worship then they are not truly following the noahide laws. But I don't believe that all Jewish scholars agree with that. Some note that modern Muslims did not invent a religion they inherited it and therefore, they are not in violation of this prohibition."

"Now interestingly," Aaron continued, "Some Muslims follow not only the seven noahide laws but also the 613 laws given by Moses to the Israelites. For that reason, there are some Jewish scholars who actually believe that these Muslims may be Jews even though they have never undergone a conversion. But I believe this is considered an extreme minority view."

"There are some Jews who believe that some Muslims could actually be Jews?" asked Al Zahra in amazement.

"Yes, there are some. The belief is that a Muslim who observes the 613 laws and the Thirteen Principles of Faith, as delineated by the Rambam, is also a Jew," said Aaron. "I had to memorize the Thirteen Principles as a child. Do you want me to recite them for you?" Aaron asked with a chuckle.

"Of course," she laughed. "I want to know if I am a Jew."

"These are the Thirteen Principles of Faith:

"1.Belief that G-d created and rules all things. Muslims believe this.

2.Belief that there is only one G-d. There is no unity or trinity or anything of that nature. He alone is G-d. Muslims believe this.

3.Belief that G-d does not have a physical body and laws of physics do not apply to Him. Thus, a man cannot be G-d and he will never take a physical form. Muslims believe this.

4.Belief that G-d is the first and the last. Muslims believe this.

5.Belief that it is proper to pray only to G-d. One should not pray to anyone or anything else. Many Muslims believe this.

6.Belief that the words of the prophets are true. This refers to the Jewish prophets. Many Muslims, though not all, believe this to be true.

7.Belief that the prophecy of Moses is true. Again many, though not all Muslims believe this to be true.

8.Belief that the entire Torah, as it exists today, is that which was given to Moses. This is where many Muslims have trouble.

They believe that the Torah was altered by the rabbis. The rabbis were strictly forbidden from altering the Torah in any way.

9.Belief that the Torah will not ever be changed and another Torah will never be given by G-d. Here again, many Muslims regard the Qur'an to be the new improved Torah just as some Christians consider the Greek Testament (what they call the New Testament) to be the new improved Torah. According to Rambam a true Jew cannot believe this. Again, this is a problem for many Muslims.

10. Belief that G-d knows all of man's deeds and thoughts. Muslims believe this.

11.Belief that G-d rewards those who keep his commandments and punishes those who do not. Muslims believe this.

12.Belief in the coming messiah. Muslims believe this though they believe in a different messiah.

13. Belief in the resurrection of the dead. I don't know what Muslims believe about this."

"So you are saying that there are some Jewish scholars who believe that a Muslim who observes the 613 laws, and believes the Thirteen Principles of Faith that you just recited, could actually be a Jew," asked Al Zahra.

"Yes, I have known a rabbi who has said this, but not publicly," replied Aaron.

"But I thought one either had to be born a Jew, or to convert to become a Jew," said Al Zahra.

"Therein is the key to his belief that a Muslim can be a Jew. Those who believe this believe that the conversion process is essentially a tool given to the rabbis to help assure that a conversion is true. In other words, the conversion to Judaism is a matter that is tested by the conversion process to assure that one has undergone a true conversion. However, conversion is a condition of the heart and one's relationship to G-d. Avram did not have a rabbi convert him yet he became Avraham and was in the covenant. According to this view, one can convert to Judaism without ever undergoing a normal conversion process if G-d places the conversion in his heart."

"Do you believe that Aaron?" asked Al Zahra.

"I don't know," he said. "I believe the biggest problem for a Muslim would be some of the Principles of Faith. For example, it is taught that the Qur'an replaced the Torah. This could not be accepted by a Jew. That does not mean that a Muslim could not believe that the Qur'an is a divinely inspired writing. It just means that he could not believe that the Qur'an replaced the Torah."

"Aaron, do you know that I believe all of the Thirteen Principles of Faith that you recited and I observe the 613 laws. I don't know if it was because I was around Jews as a child or if I learned these principles somewhere else. But I have believed all of those principles since as far back as I can remember. If some Muslims are actually Jews, then a Jewish man could marry one of these devout Muslim women and vice versa, isn't that true?" she asked.

"I don't know," Aaron replied.

Aaron and Al Zahra sat quietly looking at each other for a few moments then she said, "I better get to my class," as she stood to her feet.

"Aaron, does your family believe that Muslims can be Jews," she asked.

"My family is deceased," said Aaron. "I live with my aunt and my uncle. My father was a neurologist who graduated from this medical school."

Al Zahra said, "I am sorry to hear about your family and I would like for you to tell me about them. Do you mind if I ask how they died?"

"They were murdered," Aaron said.

"Murdered," replied Al Zahra in troubled amazement. "Who would do such a thing?"

"They were killed by Muslim terrorists in Israel," Aaron replied.

"Aaron, I am so sorry," said Al Zahra as she looked at Aaron with a troubled expression. "I hope you don't blame all Muslims for those who did this to your family."

Aaron replied, "No. I don't blame Muslims for this. I know that not all Muslims are like those men."

"Thank you Aaron," she said as she embraced him. "I will see you later."

"Ok," replied Aaron as he turned to go to his class.

Over the next several days, the events of the World Trade Center bombing unfolded. Airplanes were grounded and security at the airports was tightened. It was soon discovered that the individuals who planned the attack were Muslim terrorists. Initially, the death toll from the attack remained uncertain, but eventually it was officially determined that 2,819 people were killed in the attack on the Twin Towers.

III

It was the Thursday evening of the week before Thanksgiving. Aaron sat in the living room of his Aunt Sarah and Uncle Samuel's stately home. They were discussing plans for Thanksgiving celebration. Aaron had not yet told them about his new friend Al Zahra. Aunt Sarah asked, "Is there anyone you would like to invite to Thanksgiving dinner Aaron?"

Aaron paused momentarily before responding then finally said, "Well there is someone I thought I might invite."

"Who is it?" asked Uncle Samuel.

"A friend from school who is not Jewish," replied Aaron. "Is it okay if I invite someone who is not Jewish?" asked Aaron.

"Aaron, you know we have always opened our home to Jews as well as non-Jews. Of course, you can invite him. What is his name?" asked Uncle Samuel.

"Actually, he is a she," said Aaron. "Her family lives in Palestine and she doesn't have any place to go."

"Oh, I see," said Uncle Samuel immediately understanding the complication.

"Aaron, this isn't someone you have been dating is it?" Aunt Sarah asked.

"No, she is just a friend," said Aaron.

"I noticed you have been going out quite frequently lately. Have you been spending time with her?" Aunt Sarah asked.

"We have been studying together, that's all," said Aaron.

"You know Aaron," said Aunt Sarah, "it is difficult to have a friendship with someone of the opposite gender without becoming romantically involved. That is why friendships with non-Jews of the opposite gender are often discouraged by orthodox Jews."

"I know," said Aaron, "but we are just good friends. Don't worry Aunt Sarah, everything is under control. Just out of curiosity why are romantic relationships with non-Jews forbidden? I know that they are forbidden but I really don't know why."

Uncle Samuel answered, "Historically, we know from the Tanakh that marriages with people of other religions has caused serious complications in the lives of Jews. King Solomon is a perfect example. More recently, the problem has been much more significant in that the Jewish population is diminishing because of marriages to those within other religions which results in children who are not raised as Jews. This is the reason it is prohibited by most orthodox Jews. But, it is important to know as well that there are some orthodox groups who accept marriages with those of other religions and it has been accepted in many reformed groups for a long period of time."

"Why is it especially frowned upon in relationships with Muslims?" asked Aaron.

"Well, the Muslims and the Jews have been adverse to one another for many centuries. The root of the problem goes back thousands of years. There is a tremendous amount of animosity that has built up on both sides," replied Uncle Samuel.

"That puzzles me because when I look at the similarities between Muslims and Jews I am astounded yet, at the same time, the differences are profound as well. It is hard to understand," said Aaron.

"It probably isn't so hard when one recognizes that many Muslim Arabs are descended from Avraham through his son Ishmael. Other Muslim Arabs are descended from Avraham's grandson Esau. They share not only the DNA with the Jews but the same religious roots."

"That I understand but what I don't understand is how they developed so much hatred for one another." said Aaron.

"You brought up the Muslim people, is your friend Muslim by any chance?" asked Uncle Samuel.

"Yes, she is," said Aaron.

"What is her name?" asked Aunt Sarah.

"Al Zahra Abdul," replied Aaron.

"Wasn't Al Zahra one of the daughter's of Mohammad?" asked Aunt Sarah. "In fact, isn't she the one from whom all descendants of Mohammad claim to descend? Her name means "Lady of Light."

"Yes, that is correct. I looked up her name," replied Aaron.

"Well Aaron, you know that I have concerns about what you are doing and what consequences it might have for you. Marriages with non-Jews are discouraged in our particular branch of orthodoxy. You ultimately have to decide for yourself whether you can continue this "friendship" without becoming romantically involved and if you do become romantically involved, whether you are going to break it off," said Uncle Samuel.

Uncle Samuel paused momentarily, then continued, "As far as inviting her to our home, as I mentioned, our home is open to people of other faiths. If you are comfortable in continuing in this friendship, then you are certainly welcome to bring her here for Thanksgiving and we will treat with the same dignity and respect that we treat all of our guests."

"I agree with Samuel," said Aunt Sarah. "She is welcome to enjoy Thanksgiving with us."

"Great," said Aaron. "I am glad that you feel that way. I will invite her here."

When Thanksgiving Day arrived, Aaron drove to Al Zahra's apartment to pick her up. "I am nervous about meeting your aunt and uncle," she said as they drove down Forsyth Blvd. toward the Levy home.

"Don't be nervous," said Aaron. "You will find that they are very kind and pleasant people." Aaron's words proved true. As Uncle Samuel opened the door he said with a smile, "You must be Al Zahra."

"Yes, and you are Uncle Samuel. Aaron has told me so much about you."

"Welcome into our home," he said as she extended her hand to him.

Aunt Sarah came from the kitchen and said, "Hi, I am Sarah. It is good to meet you." She shook Al Zahra's hand and led her into the den. "Please have a seat and make yourself at home."

"Aaron tells us you are from Palestine," said Aunt Sarah. "Where in Palestine are you from?"

"I grew up in a rural area southeast of Rafah in the Gaza Strip. My father is a doctor who works at a hospital in Israel. It takes several hours to drive to the hospital so sometimes he stays there for several days then returns home. When I was a child, he often took me with him. That is when I decided I wanted to be a doctor."

"Isn't it unusual for someone from Gaza to work at a hospital in Israel," asked Uncle Samuel.

"Yes, it is very unusual," replied Al Zahra. "My father has some kind of relationship with some government officials in

Israel. I never fully understood what it was about and he always told us not to discuss it with anyone. But because of that relationship he is permitted to cross the border and practice medicine in Israel."

"That is very interesting," said Aaron. "I wonder what his connection to the Israeli government might be. I would think that would be dangerous."

"Yes, I believe it is dangerous," she replied. "As you know, there are many restrictions on relationships that a person in Gaza may have with Israelis. Yasaar Arafat is very firm on those issues. A person can receive the death sentence just for selling real estate to a Jew. It is a very sad situation. My father says that this is the dark period before the reunion of all of the brothers of Avraham. He says it will happen when Moshiach appears and causes the hatred to turn to tears of sorrow and forgiveness."

"Does your father believe there will be a day when the Jews and the Muslims will come together as brothers?" asked Aaron.

"Yes," replied Al Zahra. "He said there will be a day when the third temple will be built on the Temple Mount immediately south of the Dome of the Rock. When that happens the brothers of Avraham, the Muslims and the Jews, will embrace each other and cry tears of happiness and forgiveness."

"When will that happen?" asked Uncle Samuel.

"My father says it will happen when Moshiach/Mahdi appears to unite the sons of Avraham."

"I am fascinated by the fact that you used the term Moshiach/Mahdi. Moshiach is the Jewish messiah and Mahdi is the Muslim messiah. Yet, you use the terms as if they are one and the same. Can you explain why you use the terms in that way?" asked Uncle Samuel.

'Of course," replied Al Zahra. "According to Muslim teaching there will someday come a person who will be a messiah to the Muslim people called Mahdi. Many Muslims believe that he will be a descendant of Mohammad. But unless he is royalty there is no way to know that for sure because his descent is from a maternal line and there are very few records on female lines of descent except in the royal families. My father also says that there is a Jewish messiah who will be descended from King David by a paternal line. According to my father the Muslim Mahdi and the Jewish messiah may be one and the same."

"Wow," said Aaron. "That is fascinating. You have never told me this before. So really, your father is hoping for the arrival of the Jewish messiah who could also be the Muslim messiah. Is that right?"

"Yes, that is correct," replied Al Zahra.

Aunt Sarah smiled as if she were suddenly endowed with some insight. "Al Zahra, Mohammad had a daughter named Fatima Al Zahra from whom all descendants of Mohammad claim descent. Her name meant 'Lady of Light.' Isn't that right?"

"Yes it is," replied Al Zahra.

"Where did you get your name? Did your parents ever tell you why they named you Al Zahra?" asked Aunt Sarah.

"Yes," replied Al Zahra. "Our family is descended from Mohammad through his daughter Al Zahra. My cousin is the king of Jordan."

Aunt Sarah smiled and said, "Somehow I knew that. When Aaron first told me your name I somehow knew immediately that you were of the royal family. I am sure that there are many women in Arab nations named Al Zahra, but very few of them would have the resources to come to America to attend a private medical school. I had a hunch that before this day was over we would learn that you are of royal descent. Al Zahra, you are a very fascinating young woman. When I talk to you I almost feel as if I am talking to a Jew."

Aaron looked at Al Zahra and they both laughed.

"Ok, what is the private joke?" laughed Uncle Samuel.

"Oh, Al Zahra and I were having a conversation one day about the possibility that a Muslim who follows the 613 laws and believes the Thirteen Principles of Faith could actually be a Jew," replied Aaron.

"What? I don't think I have heard that before," said Uncle Samuel.

"Well I met a Chassidic rabbi on campus about three years ago who told me those things," replied Aaron. "He moved to Israel last year but he told me that he believes that there are thousands, if not millions, of Arab Muslims who are actually Orthodox Jews but who have never been formally converted. He said that Judaism has focused upon the formal conversion process almost as if HaShem cannot convert someone independently of a rabbi. He believes that part of the awakening in the messianic age will be a realization by Jews that there are millions of Muslim Jews throughout the world who have absolutely no knowledge that they are really Jews. I often wonder if he is correct and if so, whether Al Zahra is one of them."

Suddenly, as if out of nowhere Aunt Sarah said, "Al Zahra, I am so happy to have met you. In the short time that we have spoken I feel that my eyes have been opened to many things I did not ever believe possible. You are Aaron's friend and I can already tell that the affection between you is deep. I don't really understand precisely what is happening and whether there is a romantic relationship, and I am sure no one here fails to recognize the difficulty that would create. But I want you to know that regardless of your religion and your background, you have a family here. You will be like a daughter to us. I would never have believed this possible until I met you and heard you speak. All I can say is that you seem to give me be the ayin of

HaShem." Aaron was stunned as his aunt stood up and embraced this Muslim woman. He looked at Uncle Samuel who looked back at Aaron and chuckled with a shrug. Uncle Samuel then said, "Al Zahra, I agree with Sarah. You are family here."

The Thanksgiving celebration was a wonderful event for Al Zahra and the Levy family. They wound up playing table games well into the night. As Aaron drove Al Zahra home he asked, "So what do you think of Aunt Sarah and Uncle Samuel. I was so afraid of what they would say when they found out you are Muslim, but they were actually very "cool" about it."

"Oh Aaron," said Al Zahra. "I am so in love with your family. They are the sweetest kindest people I have ever met. That is the good news. The bad news is what this means to you and me. A huge hurdle to a romantic connection seems to have been removed. They would accept me as a daughter in law. I feel like I am staring unadulterated temptation right in the face. Have you changed your view on the idea of being romantically involved with a Muslim?"

"Stop it, you are tempting me," said Aaron with a laugh as he poked Al Zahra in the ribs. "I think that Uncle Samuel and Aunt Sarah were just saying that they will not stand in the way of whatever we decide to do. We have to decide what is right. Halachically, I cannot marry a Muslim and your faith will not allow you to marry a Jew. So why would we even become involved in a relationship?"

"I hate to break the news to you my dearest, rocket scientist, genius type, brain surgeon, nuclear IQ Aaron, but we are already in a relationship," said Al Zahra as she gently stroked Aaron's cheek with her index finger. "Now on the count of three let's all say, duh," Al Zahra said with a laugh.

"Are you sure your real name isn't Delilah," asked Aaron with a smile.

IV

It was Monday morning after the Thanksgiving break. Al Zahra and Aaron were sitting at a table in the lounge at the medical school. Aaron was reading the newspaper and Al Zahra was studying an article on human DNA and the Genome Project. Al Zahra looked up from her article and said, "I had an interesting conversation with my father this weekend Aaron. I called him on Sunday to see how the family was doing. He told me something very strange about Israel."

"What was that?" asked Aaron as he laid his newspaper on the table.

"Well, do you remember when I told you that my father has some kind of relationship with some people in the government of Israel?

"Yes," replied Aaron.

"He had to be careful how he said it because you never know who could be listening in on a telephone, but he said that his connections in the Israeli government have said that there is a prophet alive today."

With a puzzled expression Aaron asked, "A prophet?"

"Yes," replied Al Zahra. "He said that there is someone alive today who gives real prophecies just like the prophets of ancient Israel. He said that this person is very discreet in the manner in which he gives his prophecies and that he is very careful to keep his identity a secret except in very limited circles. Apparently, he first prophesied about twenty years ago when he was a very young man. At that time the prophecies were witnessed by thousands of people and very well documented by various intelligence services. But apparently, he was still in his search for understanding so he completely ceased all prophecies and lived a normal life in his profession. Then, only a very short time ago he began to prophecy again. According to my father this is very significant because most Jews believe that prophecy was sealed 2500 years ago and there was not to be another true prophet until Moshiach is alive and in the world."

"Your father told you all of this?" asked Aaron.

"Yes, according to my father his prophecies are very real and precise. They often foretell the exact day of events and sometimes the exact minute. He does not try to change events and it is not until the event occurs that what he said becomes obvious. Then those who read his prophecies are astounded."

"What kinds of things does he foretell?" asked Aaron.

"The bombing of the world trade Center for one thing," said Al Zahra. "But there is something very frightening as well. He recently foretold the death of a major leader of terrorist connection to Palestine whom he said will die from an unexplainable brain hemorrhage. He said that he will suddenly collapse then expire on November 11, 2004 and that several weeks later, on December 27, 2004 over a hundred thousand people, mostly Muslim, will be dead in the aftermath of a wave that he described as a "flying scroll" that will occur one day earlier. No one knows what he is talking about, but everyone who has knowledge of his prior prophecies is very concerned. He has now foretold what some say is a clear prophecy of the death of the pope and another catastrophic event involving what he calls the "Havana Winds." Many believe he is referring to a hurricane in the southeast part of the United States or Cuba."

"That is very strange," said Aaron as he noticed that an elderly person at the table next to them seem to be listening intently, albeit discreetly.

"The strangest part is that he does not live in Israel though he is a Jew. I understand that most Jews believe that when either the prophet Elijah or the Moshiach first appears he will appear in Israel. But this person does not live in Israel. In fact Aaron, according to my father's sources, he has some connection to this university. Do you know anything about this at all?"

"Actually, I recall my father saying something about that when I was very young. In fact, the reason our family took our trip to Israel where they died was because my father said that he had personally witnessed some prophecies. I remember Uncle Samuel and my father talking about it. They were very excited and they said it means we are at the time of the arrival of Moshiach. I never heard my uncle mention it again after my family was killed."

Aaron noticed that the man at the next table who had been eavesdropping had dialed someone on his cell phone. Aaron overheard him say, "The Palestinians know about it…" Aaron could not hear the rest of the conversation. Suddenly the elderly man said, "I will take care of it right away, in the mean time set up the meeting at the Pentagon." He stood up abruptly and walked at a rapid pace out of the lounge and into hall.

"What was that all about," asked Al Zahra. "He acted like he was very disturbed about what I said."

"I don't know but we better get to class," said Aaron as he stood to his feet. "I will ask Uncle Samuel what it was that he and my father were discussing that day before we went to Israel."

As Al Zahra and Aaron walked down the hall toward their class, Aaron could not stop thinking about the conversation he had overheard as a very young child. "Why didn't Uncle Samuel ever talk about it again after his family's death?" Aaron wondered. "Why did he remain so quiet for all of these years?"

Later that same day Al Zahra received notification from her professor that she was needed in the dean's office. Puzzled by the request she walked to the office with concern that something may have happened to one of her family members. She was invited by the secretary into the office where she was greeted by the dean and a well dressed man and a woman.

"Good afternoon, Ms. Abdul," said the dean, "This is Paul Strauss and Sandra Johnson. They are with the National Security Agency and they would like to speak with you for a few moments in private. You are not required to meet with them. And they have told me that you are not in any trouble but they would like to ask you some questions. Is that agreeable to you?"

"Oh, sure," replied Al Zahra.

"Ok, then I will excuse myself so you can speak freely," said the dean as he left the room.

"How can I help you?" asked Al Zahra.

"Ms. Abdul," said Mr. Strauss, "yesterday you made a telephone call to your father at a hospital in Israel. During that telephone conversation your father disclosed some information to you that is vital to the national security of both Israel and the United States. The reason that we have asked to speak to you is that we have reason to believe that you and your family could be placed in danger by the communication of this information."

"How do you know about that telephone call?" asked Al Zahra.

Mr. Strauss reached into his pocket and pulled out a digital recording device which he turned on for just a few seconds revealing to Al Zahra that the conversation had been recorded in its entirety.

"Why would you record that telephone conversation?" asked Al Zahra.

"Ms. Abdul, the NSA has been observing your activities since you came to the United States six years ago," said Ms. Johnson.

"Why would you do that?" Al Zahra asked.

"We have done that because of your prominent position in the royal families of the Arab nations of the Middle East," said Ms. Johnson. "The bottom line is that even though you don't think of yourself as such, you are an Arab Princess. Neither you nor your family has ever been considered a threat to the United States but we have been concerned for your safety for several reasons. First and foremost, we have concern because your family's prominence places you in a position of danger. That is simply by virtue of who you are. The second reason is not quite so altruistic. We have concern that if something were to happen to you while in the United States, it could have serious international ramifications. Lastly, although we do not consider you a threat to the United States, you do live in Palestine which is not friendly to the United States or its ally Israel. Therefore, there is some concern that you could inadvertently transfer information, of which you could come into possession, to the leaders of Palestine that could threaten the security of the United States or Israel. For these reasons, your activities have been monitored on a daily basis since you came here. By monitoring your communications we learned that your father has come into possession of such information which he subsequently communicated to you in the telephone conversation yesterday."

"When we are monitoring you," said Mr. Strauss, "our objective is to be the least intrusive as we can possibly be. Generally, our effort is to insure your safety without disturbing you. In fact, that is the reason we are talking to you now. Yesterday when you discussed the matter of "the prophet" with your father, you became informed of information that is considered classified. We listened carefully to see if you would repeat the information you had learned or if you would dismiss it as nonsense. Unfortunately, you chose to repeat this information to your boyfriend Aaron. For that reason, we are contacting you to request that you not discuss this matter of the prophet with anyone else."

"So the information about the prophet is true?" asked Al Zahra in amazement.

Ms. Johnson smiled at Al Zahra. "Let me put it this way, we would not reveal our identities as NSA agents unless there were a very good reason. That is why we must request that you not discuss this with anyone else. We must also ask that you request Aaron to say nothing further of this. Your knowledge of this information places you in grave danger. I am sure your father didn't realize this when he told you about 'the prophet' but there are those who would torture or kill anyone who possesses this knowledge in order to learn more information or to destroy the evidence. Either way the result is the same. Your safety is compromised."

"So the elderly gentleman at the table next to Aaron and I this morning is with the NSA?" asked Al Zahra.

"Well, actually no. He is retired from the British Secret Service. He works for us on contract on relatively low risk activities such as monitoring a princess from an Arab nation. Well, at least until now it was low risk but there is a certain amazing lady from Palestine who has suddenly raised the stakes," laughed Mr. Strauss with a wink.

"You will have to excuse my partner," interrupted Ms. Johnson as she nudged Mr. Strauss with her elbow. "That is his way of telling you he is impressed with you which, if I know Paul means first and foremost he is probably impressed with your striking beauty."

"Ok, if I didn't know better I would think this is some kind of joke," said Al Zahra. "This sounds like a Tom Clancy novel."

"I assure you Ms. Abdul…" Mr. Strauss paused, "Do you mind if I call you Al Zahra?"

"Of course not," replied Al Zahra. "May I call you Paul?"

"Absolutely," replied Mr. Strauss.

"And you can call me Sandy," said Ms. Johnson with a smile.

"As I was saying," continued Mr. Strauss, "this is not a joke. It is a very serious matter. Are you willing to agree that you will not discuss 'the prophet' further with anyone in the United States or Palestine, except of course your immediate family but only in person and not via telephone or internet?"

"May I discuss it with Aaron?" asked Al Zahra.

"We don't want to tell you what you what you can and cannot discuss with those closest to you such as Aaron or your own family. We are simply asking that you be very discreet in any future communications of this nature. The most important thing is that we do not want this information to become widely known. You are a very intelligent woman and I am sure that we don't have to explain the seriousness of this matter. Do we have your word that you will keep this in strictest confidence?" asked Mr. Strauss.

"Yes, you have my word. But can you tell me a little about this prophet?" asked Al Zahra.

"The less you know the better for you and everyone else. This information will probably become public in a little while, but for the time being less knowledge is better. But if you have some specific questions I will tell you if we can answer them," said Ms. Johnson. "Understand that we are not saying this is true. We are simply saying that there is a person whom many within various intelligence services around the world believe has the ability to prophesy."

"Is it true that he is a descendant of King David?" asked Al Zahra.

Ms. Johnson looked at Mr. Strauss then nodded her head very slightly.

Mr. Strauss said, "According to genealogical records maintained by various governments throughout history, including the United States, the subject is a patrilineal descendant of King David through his son Solomon."

"Is he a Jew?" asked Al Zahra.

"Yes, much like Moses who was born a Jew but raised in the religions of Egypt, he was born a Jew and raised in both Christianity and Judaism. He was taught both Christianity and Judaism," said Mr. Strauss. "I can anticipate your next question," said Mr. Strauss. "Is he the Moshiach ben David?"

"Well yes, that is my next question. And also, if not, is he considered dangerous in any way?" asked Al Zahra.

"As a matter of fact," said Ms. Johnson, "I am a Christian and Mr. Strauss is a Jew. Of course, Christians believe that the messiah was J'sus who came long ago. However, many Christians also believe that it is possible that a descendant of King David will appear and fulfill some of the messianic prophecies before the return of J'sus. This question has been posed to many leading Christian scholars around the world who have considered the possibility that he might be this prophesied descendant of King David. There are of course others who are convinced that he is the person identified as the antichrist in the Book of Revelation of the Christian Bible."

"Is that what you believe?" asked Al Zahra as she looked inquisitively at Ms. Johnson.

"I'm afraid I haven't decided yet," replied Ms. Johnson. "For me the jury is still out. However, having studied the history of this man in tremendous detail, I am convinced that at least for now, he poses no threat to anyone with the possible exception of terrorists and those who violate human and civil rights. That seems to be his 'hot button.' He becomes very upset with terrorists organizations and oppressive governmental regimes including sometimes our own. But I will say that in some cases, his prophecies look more like commandments or judgments than they do foreknowledge. That has many of us at the NSA very concerned. Particularly since when he does this no known crime is being committed. And what court could ever convict someone for verbally commanding the death of a known terrorist by a brain hemorrhage and setting the date for the occurrence when the death is not the result of any human hand? If one of his recent "prophecies" occurs, that is precisely what is going to happen. But even if no crime is being committed, it is extremely frightening to realize that someone could possess such power."

"Of course, as a Jew," said Mr. Strauss, I have to take very seriously the possibility that he is indeed Moshiach ben David. Most reformed Jews in America had given up on the idea that Moshiach could be a real person. However, all of that changed when this fellow showed up with the proper pedigree, intelligence and apparent supernatural powers. As a Jew I am very seriously considering the possibility that he is indeed Moshiach ben David."

"What does he do for a living," asked Al Zahra.

"I am sorry but that we cannot tell you," replied Ms. Johnson. "We can't really tell you anything that might lead to the disclosure of his identity. I can tell you that although he travels throughout the world, he still lives in the United States. There probably isn't much else that we can tell you about him at this time."

"Ok, let me ask you just one more question," said Al Zahra. "Who does he say he is? Does he say he is the Jewish messiah Moshiach ben David?"

"Actually, that is very interesting," said Ms. Johnson. "He won't say who he is. Many people have asked him about his prophecies and he acts as though he doesn't know what they are talking about. In fact, he even acts like they are silly for suggesting that he has prophesied. We know that he has a very small group of people with whom he has shared some of his prophetic abilities based upon some of his emails we have intercepted. But it appears that they are probably less than a half dozen in number. In fact, it appears that those closest to him, including his business partner and his own family do not even know. That is probably for their safety."

"Thank you for taking the time to talk to us, Al Zahra," said Mr. Strauss. "Hopefully, we won't ever have to bother you again."

"Thank you for explaining the situation to me," said Al Zahra. "Actually, it is a little comforting to know that someone is watching out for my safety. The intrusion into privacy is a little unnerving though. Incidentally, you don't have any cameras in my apartment or anything like that, do you?"

"No," said Ms. Johnson. "We would not infringe upon your personal privacy in any indecent way."

"Thank you," said Al Zahra. "It was nice to meet both of you."

"You are welcome, Al Zahra," said Mr. Strauss as he gave his card to Al Zahra. "Here is my card. Call me if you ever have any concerns about anything."

"I will," said Al Zahra as she exited the office.

"Goodbye, Al Zahra," said Ms. Johnson. "It has been a real pleasure and honor to meet you. Even though we met under peculiar circumstances, I will always consider this one of the high points of my life."

Surprised by the comment Al Zahra turned around and said, "Thank you. That was very kind of you. This conversation will also be something that I will never forget." Al Zahra turned and walked out of the office.

V

It was the evening after Shabbat, on December 22nd, 2001, the beginning of the week of winter break. Aaron was teaching his Krav Maga class when Al Zahra entered the room. Aaron's Krav Maga classes were quite popular on campus. He had long ago acquired a black belt in Tae Kwon Do, the Korean martial arts, and thereafter a black belt in Krav Maga, the popular Israeli fighting technique. He had developed a system that combined both disciplines which had been publicized in the local newspapers and had become well known in St. Louis. He generally had at least 100 students in each of his classes.

As Aaron explained a method for disarming a knife attacker, Al Zahra watched with feigned interest. Aaron saw her from the corner of his eye and smiled. He then asked his assistant to continue the demonstration and walked over to Al Zahra.

"Thank you for stopping by Al Zahra," he said.

"You acted as if something was bothering you," replied Al Zahra. "You said we need to talk about our relationship and where it is going. Aaron, is everything alright?"

"Let me get my jacket and we can go somewhere where we can talk," he said.

"Aaron, what is wrong," asked Al Zahra with distress clearly revealed in her voice.

"Come on, we will talk about it," he replied.

As they walked down the hall then out onto the snow covered campus Aaron said, "Al Zahra, I am really concerned that we have gotten too close emotionally. I really feel that we need to take a break from each other so we can clear our thoughts."

"Aaron, somehow I knew you were going to say that," she said. "Why are you doing this now? It is too late for this. We are in too deep. Please Aaron, think about what you are saying. It was just a month ago that we had such a wonderful time at your house for Thanksgiving."

"I know, Al Zahra and I am so sorry. Do you remember what you said to me when I was driving you back to your apartment? You said that we are already in a relationship. That is the problem. We can't be in a relationship. We are from two different worlds. Al Zahra, I am falling in love with you and you are falling in love with me. It is a forbidden relationship. We have to break it off now before it is too late."

"Aaron, you don't get it," she screamed as tears formed in her eyes. "It is already too late. I am already in love with you. Please think about what you are saying Baby."

Aaron took Al Zahra in his arms and held her close as she trembled and cried. "I have thought about it for a long time," he said. "We can't be romantically involved."

"Okay, then we won't be romantically involved. We will be just friends. We can do that Aaron. But we can't stop seeing each other. That will be too hard. That will be like dying."

"That won't work Al Zahra. You and I both know it. We have to cut it off."

"Is that how you really feel Aaron? Are you saying that this friendship of love we have developed over the last four months is so meaningless that you can just throw it away? I can't do that. If you want to throw it away then that is your decision and your decision alone."

Aaron replied, "I am sorry Al Zahra. We have no choice. The quicker we can terminate this relationship the better. I know this is really hard for you. Let me drive you home in your car then I will take a cab back to campus and pick up my car."

"Don't bother and don't flatter yourself. Do you think I can't get over you? I will be over you so fast your head will spin and I won't look back. In fact, I am already over you," Al Zahra said as she turned and walked quickly toward her car. She stopped then shouted back at Aaron, "I just hope in ten years when you look back at this moment you don't say, 'That was the worst mistake of my life.'"

"Al Zahra, wait a minute," said Aaron. Al Zahra turned and ran toward the parking lot, got into her car and drove quickly out into the street. Her visibility impaired by her tears she nearly collided with a Jaguar S Type as she sped down Lindell Blvd. weaving in and out of traffic not really knowing where she was driving. She drove about aimlessly for two hours then finally arrived at her apartment where she found six voice messages from Aaron. All of them asked if she was alright but none of them offered to reunite. "Meaningless messages," thought Al Zahra as she wiped the tears from her eyes, "meaningless messages."

As Aaron drove home after his break up with Al Zahra, he felt a strange lump in his throat and a tearing sensation in the pit of his stomach. He arrived at his aunt and uncle's house and pulled into the driveway where he sat with the engine off listening repeatedly to "Yerushalayim Shel Zahav" (Jerusalem of Gold) performed by Israeli singer Ofra Haza. This had become the favorite song of Al Zahra and Aaron.

Aaron noticed a strange sensation that he had not felt since he attended his family's funeral at the age of five. His eyes burned and his throat felt dry and scratchy. Suddenly he felt his chest heaving as if he could not get enough oxygen. His face felt warm and he noticed that something wet was moving down his cheek causing a tickling sensation. In amazement he touched his face with his hand and discovered tears rolling gently down his cheek. He began gasping for air as he began crying "Al Zahra, Al Zahra. Beautiful, precious Al Zahra. Why did you ask to borrow my anatomy book? Why couldn't you have ignored me that day? Why couldn't you have been a Jew? Why can't I stop loving you? HaShem help us please. Comfort Al Zahra tonight. Help her get through this. And please HaShem, help me too." Aaron laid his hands on the steering wheel of his BMW, rested his head on his hands and cried for nearly an hour. He didn't even know that he still knew how to cry. He had not cried since he was five years old. Al Zahra was right. Breaking up was like dying.

That night Al Zahra stayed up until 2:00 am hoping that Aaron would make one of his late night calls and tell her that he had made a terrible mistake. "Please Aaron, just call. If you call, I will answer," she thought to herself. The next morning Al Zahra was planning to leave for Palestine. Aaron was supposed to drive her to the airport but as Al Zahra anticipated, he didn't show up to take her, nor did he call. She had waited an extra half hour hoping that Aaron would show up and say that he had made a bad mistake. Al Zahra was going home for the winter break to be with her family. As she walked through the airport she noticed the colored lights and holiday decorations. They seemed so empty and vain to her. She sat at the gate as she waited to board her plane to Palestine. Her stomach muscles were sore from crying and her face and eyes were red, tight and dry. There were no more tears left to be shed. Playing in her portable CD player was "Jerusalem of Gold." The plane boarded and she departed for Lebanon in route to Palestine.

As the plane flew over the shoreline into Gaza Al Zahra looked out the window into the sunny sky. Gaza International Airport was unusually busy because of the many holiday travelers. "Maybe Aaron is right," she thought. "This world is not for Aaron. He could not even come home to meet my family without risking death or serious bodily harm." As Al Zahra got off the plane and entered the airport her father and her mother were there to great her. When she saw them she began running and embraced them with tears but she didn't tell them about Aaron. She could not bring herself to tell them that she had been so emotionally devastated by someone she loved so much, particularly a Jew.

During Al Zahra's first three nights in Gaza she stayed at home talking with her family. On the third night she sat with her family in the den of their beautiful home. Her brother Mansoor asked, "So, Al Zahra, what do you think of the Americans? Are they beginning to understand the plight of the Palestinians? Have you met any Jews? I know you have. What are American Jews like?"

"Yes, I have met some Jews. They are Americanized. They don't seem to think exactly the way Israeli Jews think," she replied.

"What do you mean?" asked Mansoor.

"Well for one thing, they don't seem to be as emotionally attached to the struggles that took place in Israel during the last century. As a result, I think they are better prepared to look for solutions to the problem rather than escalate it. Also, Americans went through something not totally unlike our current conflict with the Israelis. From the time the colonies were established in the 1600's until the Civil War, Americans had slavery. The result was that in the latter part of the 19th century and well into the 20th century, there was tremendous hatred between the black people and the white people. But there was a president named John F. Kennedy who believed that they could get past the conflict without bloodshed. Working with a black man named Martin Luther King, he was able to establish inroads into freedom for all people. John F. Kennedy presented the Civil Rights Act of 1957 which was not adopted until 1964 after Kennedy had been assassinated. The result of his effort is that today, black people and white people are considered equal. But the most interesting part of this is that the strongest supporters of the Civil Rights Act of 1964 were Jews. I almost never hear a Jew in Israel saying that Palestinians should be treated equally with Jews. It seems that we are discriminated against not because of a valid religious difference between our people and the Jews but because we are seen as a threat to the Jews. Think about it. In a democracy what would happen if all Arab Muslims were allowed back into Israel? The Jews would be outnumbered and would completely lose control very quickly as a result of elections. I have a Jewish friend named Aaron who says that the problem is that there was not supposed to be a democracy in Israel. There is supposed to be a constitutional monarchy when the time was right. But that time has not yet arrived. When it does, there will be no more conflict between the Muslims and the Jews."

"You have a Jewish friend?" asked Mansoor. "Does he treat you as an equal or does he look down on you?"

Al Zahra's lips quivered as she answered, "He treats me as more than his equal. He is the kindest person I have ever known. He treats me like a princess but he will not deny his religious convictions and when it appears that he might, he gently asks my forgiveness as he takes time away from me."

"What are you talking about," asked Mansoor. "Who is this guy? Is he a boyfriend?"

Al Zahra responded "He is just someone I know. I am getting tired I think I will retire now."

Al Zahra's father said, "Very well. Tomorrow we will take a trip into the Municipality of Gaza. I have some interesting things to show you."

"Ok, father," said Al Zahra as she gave him a good night embrace. "Good night Mama."

Al Zahra's mother responded as she embraced her daughter, "Good night my precious child. It is good to have you home."

The next morning Al Zahra's father knocked on her bedroom door and said, "Are you up yet? We have a big day ahead of us."

"Yes, I am awake," replied Al Zahra wiping the sleep out of her eyes.

"Al Zahra, would you mind too much if I asked you to wear your traditional clothes today. Things have gotten a little tense in Gaza Municipality lately. I will explain as we drive."

"Oh yuk," said Al Zahra. "I suppose if I have to," she said with a laugh.

"I think it would be a good idea," said Dr. Abdul. His sober tone momentarily gave Al Zahra chills.

"Is everything ok, Daddy," she asked. "What happened? Did Hamas take over?"

"There have been some problems. I will tell you about it on the ride to the city."

Al Zahra felt a sickening feeling in her stomach as she put on the hijab (headscarf.) She felt like she needed to vomit. "I feel wrapped up like a Tootsie Roll," she thought as she looked in the mirror at the full length dress and the black hijab.

As they left the house Al Zahra's mother said, "Be careful. I will have a nice dinner prepared when you return from Gaza Municipality."

"Bye mama," said Al Zahra as she gave her mother a hug.

"We will be back before dark," said Dr. Abdul.

As they drove down the highway in the family Mercedes Al Zahra asked, "What is going on Daddy? Why did you want me to wear the traditional clothes today? I always wore blue jeans and a sweat shirt or a tee-shirt before I left for America. What happened?"

"Things are different now," said Dr. Abdul. He pulled the car over to the side of the road and said, "Let's get out so we can talk for a little while and I will tell you what is happening."

Al Zahra and her father got out of the vehicle and began walking along the side of the dusty road. "Daddy, I know something is wrong. I am a big girl now. You can tell me," she said.

"Okay," said Dr. Abdul. "Things are a lot different than they were a few years ago. Hamas has become very powerful. They are killing everyone who gets in their path and they are openly challenging Fatah and Arafat. Arafat is supporting them to avoid a coup. But the situation is very serious. I have something very sad to tell you and it will hurt you. I have been trying to find the right time to tell you and I didn't want to tell you at home or while we were driving. That is why I stopped."

Al Zahra turned toward her father with great trepidation and said, "Okay, I am ready. What is it?"

Her father took her in his arms and pulled her to him in an embrace and said, "Do you remember who you used to play with as a child?"

"Yes," she replied. I played with Basha'ir and Hawadah Ghayeb. When I was 14 you told me that I could not spend time with them anymore because they were training to become Shaheed (martyrs) for Islam."

"Yes, that's true. This will be hard for you to understand, Al Zahra, but Basha'ir is deceased and Hawadah is even worse. Al Zahra, there is a great evil in the land of Islam. Shaheed is encouraged by millions of people within our faith. They are teaching their children to kill themselves as suicide bombers. This is a sick perverted evil hatred and it permeates the highest level officials of Palestine. Yassar Arafat is a supporter of this evil activity and has even offered $25,000.00 rewards to surviving families of suicide bombers."

Al Zahra was visibly shaken. "Oh no," she said having heard nothing after "Basha'ir is deceased and Hawadah is even worse." She pulled away from her father and put her hands to her head and began to cry. "I can't believe that Basha'ir is gone. She was my best friend as a child." Al Zahra paused for a few moments as she felt that same sickening feeling she felt earlier when she put on the traditional clothing. She then wiped the tears from her eyes and said, "You know that is so strange that Arafat is so evil because in America he is portrayed as a hero," replied Al Zahra.

"I know that too," said her father. "It is the naïve Americans and Europeans who blindly support such an evil man in their efforts to find peace at any price. They are even willing to forfeit all that is fair and just in order to achieve peace. Arafat is the nephew of the man who was most influential in persecuting Jews in Israel and in Europe during the Holocaust. Arafat took over that man's mission but in an effort to placate him, the American government treats him like a hero. Meanwhile, those of us in Palestine under his evil rule suffer just like the Jews in Israel who suffer from his terrorism. What happened to the true heroes of the world? These men are not heroes. They are cowards. The world today is ruled by cowards. I would give anything to see one man who has the courage to stand up and expose Arafat for the evil man that he truly is."

"What happened to Basha'ir and Hawadah?" asked Al Zahra.

Dr. Abdul paused for a moment then said, "Basha'ir achieved what she thought was her Shaheed. Last year she went into Jersusalem wearing a 25 pound bomb. She killed herself along with four Israeli women, two children and one baby."

Al Zahra shook her head in disbelief then she asked, "And what happened to Hawadah?"

"Hawadah refused to pursue the Shaheed. Like you she dressed like a westerner in blue jeans and t-shirts and she refused to participate in Shaheed training classes. Several weeks ago her brother, who is a leader in Hamas, asked her to bring some food to his apartment. When she arrived she was kidnapped by her brother and several members of Hamas. They accused her of immorality and indecency for not becoming a suicide bomber and for dressing like a westerner in blue jeans. That is the reason I asked you to wear the traditional Muslim garb today," said Dr. Abdul.

"What did they do to her?" asked Al Zahra.

"Four days ago she was dumped from the back of a pick up truck naked and burned over 80% of her body," said her father. "She was able to talk and she told us what happened. She said she was raped repeatedly by many men. When they got tired of her they poured gasoline on her and set her a fire. They laughed as she burned. She was tied to a bed while this occurred. She said she lost consciousness several times from the pain. After they had finished with this 'torture' they beat her with wooden sticks then poured gasoline over her body and face and again set her afire. All this time she was still tied to the bed. Finally, after letting her burn for what she thought was several minutes, they poured scalding hot salt water over her to put out the fire and said they would let her live for two reasons. The first was because her brother was a high ranking official in Hamas and it would disgrace him for her to die this way and secondly because she would be a reminder to the rest of the women of Gaza of what would happen to women who are immoral and who wear blue jeans and mock what Hamas says is the way of A'lah. Hawadah was a very beautiful women before they did this to her. Now she is scarred beyond recognition and will be grotesquely disfigured for the rest of her life."

Al Zahra kept walking around the car trying to grasp what she had just heard. Finally, she asked, "Is there something you really wanted to show me in Gaza Municipality or were you just trying to get me out of the house so we could talk."

"I really did want to show you something if you feel that you are up to it after everything that I told you."

"Actually, it would probably help me get my mind off of what happened," she replied. "I would be up for it."

As Al Zahra and her father drove into Gaza, Al Zahra noticed dozens of hooded men walking around with assault rifles. All of the women were wearing traditional clothing and sadness seemed to feel the air. Finally, Dr. Abdul stopped at a building under construction.

"What is this going to be?" asked Al Zahra.

"Al Zahra, I do not want you to return to Gaza when you finish medical school. I would like you to stay in America so that you can live a full life in safety and comfort. I am not showing this to you to persuade you to return to Gaza, but I want you to see this." Dr. Abdulla paused for a moment then said, "Do you remember when I told you about the person called 'the prophet' in our telephone conversation?"

"Yes," replied Al Zahra.

"This hospital is being built by an anonymous donor. Everyone thinks the donor is Arafat. In reality, the donor is 'the prophet.' He does not want anyone to know that the money for this hospital is coming from a Jew. No one here knows that either. It is being funneled through some very powerful people who see the current regime in Palestine for the evil that it really is. They are working with certain individuals within Israel to bring the Moshiach/Mahdi. They believe that he might be 'the prophet.' I wanted you to know about this so that if something happens to me and you decide to return to Palestine, you will have a hospital where people will be sympathetic to your views."

Al Zahra looked at the incomplete structure and knew that the construction was far superior than anything that is ordinarily built in Gaza. "The prophet is certainly an amazing man," she thought to herself.

For Aaron the winter break seemed to last forever. He tried to occupy his time with reading and practicing martial arts. When it was time to go back to school, Aaron wondered what it would be like to see Al Zahra again. What would she say when she saw him? Would she even act like she was happy to see him or would she ignore him? He couldn't really blame her if she chose to ignore him. After all, it was pretty brutal the way he ended the relationship but he did what he felt he had to do. As Aaron walked along the snowy sidewalk across campus he could not stop thinking about Al Zahra. "I hope you are okay tonight," he thought. "Life can be such a struggle."

When classes resumed Aaron expected to see Al Zahra in the hallways or in a class. By the third day of classes he became concerned because he had not yet seen her. Aaron went to the dean's office to see if he could find out what where Al Zahra was. "Hello Aaron," said Kathleen who worked in the dean's office. "How is everything going so far this semester?"

"Its going well," said Aaron, "except for one thing."

"What is that?" asked Kathleen.

"I haven't seen Al Zahra this semester. I am really getting concerned. Has she called in?"

"We are worried too Aaron. We haven't heard from her," said Kathleen with a concerned expression on her face.

"If you hear anything will you let me know?" asked Aaron.

"I will," said Kathleen. "But aren't you in contact with her?"

"No, we decided to break off our close friendship because it was turning into a romantic relationship."

"And that is bad, why?" asked Kathleen. "Aaron, are you thinking clearly here? Everyone knows how close you were. If you love her, and everyone in the whole school knows you do, you better wake up and do something about it or she will be gone forever. It's none of my business, but I am just saying…" said Kathleen shaking her head.

That evening Aaron decided to try to call Al Zahra on her cell phone. When Al Zahra was in town they didn't usually use the cell phone because the connection was not as clear as a land line. Aaron called the cellular service to find out how to place an international call and to obtain the country code for Palestine. After he had obtained this information he placed a call to Al Zahra. As Aaron dialed the phone, someone answered in Arabic.

"Hello," said Aaron. "Is this Al Zahra?"

"Aaron," said the voice on the other end. "Why are you calling me?"

"We are concerned about you, said Aaron. You didn't come back to class after the break. When are you coming back?"

After a long pause of silence Al Zahra said, "I have decided to not come back, Aaron."

"Why?" asked Aaron.

"I can't. I have decided that being a doctor is not for me after all. I am just going to stay here in Gaza and be with my family."

"But Al Zahra, you always told me you dreamed of becoming a doctor and returning to Gaza to help your people," said Aaron.

"I know Aaron, but things have changed. I am not strong enough to go forward with those plans," she said.

"It is because of what happened between us isn't it Al Zahra?" asked Aaron.

Al Zahra didn't respond but Aaron could hear her crying.

"Isn't it Al Zahra?" asked Aaron again.

"Aaron, you really hurt me. I just can't go on right now."

"Al Zahra, you are making a bad mistake. You are just upset because we broke up but don't let that ruin your life," said Aaron.

"I'm sorry, Aaron but I have to go," she said. Then she whispered, "I love you Aaron," and she hung up the phone.

Aaron stood stunned still holding the cell phone in his hand. "I have destroyed Al Zahra's life," he thought. "Before she met me she was well on her way to becoming a great doctor. Now she has dropped out of medical school. I have done a terrible thing to her."

Aaron was so distressed that he did not even go to his classes that day. He went home and lay down on the couch experiencing the same sensations that he experienced that night he first broke up with Al Zahra. His eyes were dry and his throat was scratchy, his chest began gasping for air and he felt the warm wet substance trickling down his cheek. Only this time, he knew what it was.

Nearly a week had passed since Aaron's telephone call to Al Zahra. Aaron found that he couldn't concentrate on his studies and he couldn't sleep at night he was so distraught over the situation with Al Zahra. Finally, he decided I have to do something to get her back to medical school. I can't just destroy her life and walk away. He decided that he would call her again.

"Al Zahra, this is Aaron," he said when he reached her on the cell phone again.

"Hi Aaron," she replied. "How are your classes?"

"Al Zahra, I know that I have really hurt you and it is because of me that you have dropped out of medical school. Everyone wants you to come back. We all know you belong here."

"Aaron, I just can't come back. It is all behind me and I have to move on," she said.

"Al Zahra," said Aaron. "I need you here."

"Aaron, you are the one who said we had to break it off."

"I know," replied Aaron. "But I said that it would be a break from each other. I didn't say we couldn't get back together as friends. Before we were seeing each other every day but if we just got together a couple of times per week maybe we would be alright as friends."

"Aaron, I asked if we could be friends and you said no."

"I know and I am sorry, Al Zahra. I just needed time to think," replied Aaron.

Al Zahra said nothing for approximately thirty seconds then she said, "I am sorry Aaron. It was nice to hear from you but you really shouldn't call me anymore. It is really hard for me after we hang up. Okay?"

After several seconds of silence Aaron finally said, "Okay, Al Zahra. If you are sure that is what you want."

"No Aaron, it is not what I want but that is how it has to be now. Bye Aaron," she said softly.

"Bye Al Zahra," he replied as he heard her hang up the phone.

The following week Aaron was sitting at a table in the café where he and Al Zahra were on the morning of the bombing of the World Trade Center. He had not slept well in days. He could not stop thinking about the wonderful times they had together joking and laughing while they studied. As he sat at the table drinking his tea his thoughts were again on Al Zahra and how much he missed her. He wondered if he would ever see her again. As he read his book absently, Aaron felt someone bump into the table. "Excuse me," she said. Aaron continued to read his book. Then he noticed that the person who had bumped into the table didn't leave. Without looking up at the face of the person standing there Aaron looked at her shoes which looked strangely familiar. Suddenly he heard the words, "Do you mind if I borrow your anatomy book."

Aaron looked up and saw beautiful Al Zahra. He immediately jumped to his feet and embraced her. No words were spoken for a long time. There was no need to say anything. They just stood and embraced in silence.

Finally, Aaron asked, "Why are you here?"

"Because I thought about everything you said and I decided that being friends is better than nothing at all so I registered for classes. I am back in school."

"So you want to be friends after all?" asked Aaron.

"Yes, I think if we limit our time together to once per week we should be okay as long as you don't hurt me like that again you bonehead?" laughed Al Zahra."

"I promise I won't do that again," replied Aaron. "I learned my lesson."

Al Zahra and Aaron tried to limit their time together and were successful at first but within three weeks they were seeing each other even more frequently than before Al Zahra left for Palestine.

VI

Al Zahra held the scalpel in her right hand as she slowly made an incision in the abdomen of the male cadaver. She carefully retracted the flap and slid her gloved fingers into the abdominal cavity. "This is pretty gross," said Monica an attractive second year medical student.

"You better get used to it," said Dr. Grossman who, unbeknownst to Monica, had just approached the table behind her.

"I didn't mean anything by that," Monica said nervously.

"Part of our responsibility in treating human illnesses requires that we do things that most would consider disgusting. It is the nature of our profession," replied Dr. Grossman as he walked away.

Later that day, as they were leaving the lab, Monica asked Al Zahra, "Do you think that Dr. Grossman was annoyed with what I said about the procedure being gross?"

"No, I don't think so. I think he probably thought it was pretty gross too," laughed Al Zahra. "You are in your second year aren't you?" she asked.

"Yes," replied Monica.

"What are you planning to do when you graduate," asked Al Zahra.

"I am going to the mission field in Brazil," she replied.

"The mission field; is that something you are doing through your church?" asked Al Zahra.

"Yes," replied Monica. "I am a Presbyterian. My father is a minister and I decided long ago to devote my life to G-d by working to heal the sick in depressed parts of the world. You are from the Middle East aren't you?"

"Yes, I am from Palestine. I came to the United States to do my undergraduate work at UCLA and I stayed here for medical school. Have you met my friend Aaron Levy?"

"No, but I know who he is. Isn't he your boyfriend? I always see you together."

"Oh, I only wish," laughed Al Zahra. "I love him with all my heart but ours is a forbidden love. You see, he is a Jew and I am a Muslim. Both of our religions forbid marriage with the other."

"Oh, that is sad," said Monica. "Couldn't one of you convert?"

"Both of our religions prohibit converting just to be with someone romantically. Besides, I could never convert from my faith. My family would be devastated and I would feel that I betrayed the faith of my people. I am sure it is the same for Aaron. So, we just love each other and suffer in silent devastating anguish," said Al Zahra with a forced laugh.

"That sounds horrible," said Monica. "I couldn't stand being in love when I can't do anything about it."

"We didn't plan it that way. It just happened. But you know, it is worth the pain. We have such a wonderful wholesome friendship which is what G-d gave to us. You would be amazed though how much we talk about G-d when we are together," said Al Zahra. "In fact, you should join us some time. I am sure Aaron wouldn't mind. We have fascinating conversations. I would be curious to hear what he says about Christianity. We have never really talked about that."

"That would be interesting," said Monica. "I have never heard a Jew's view of Christianity before."

"Why don't you join us for dinner this Saturday evening then," asked Al Zahra. "I can let Aaron know you are coming."

"I would really enjoy that," replied Monica. "Where should we meet and at what time should we meet?"

"We like to have dinner at David's in Creve Coeur. We usually go about 8:30 in the evening on Saturday. That allows us to complete Shabbat. Do you want to meet us there?"

"Yes, I know where it is. I have seen it. I would love to meet you there," replied Monica. "This is very interesting for me. I am also looking forward to meeting Aaron."

"Ok then. Aaron will be delighted. We will see you on Saturday evening at 8:30 at David's in Creve Coeur."

Al Zahra and Aaron arrived at David's that Saturday evening at approximately 8:30 pm. Aaron was driving his silver BMW. As they pulled up to the curb Al Zahra asked, "Aaron, does your uncle know that you are going out with me tonight?"

"Yes," replied Aaron. "Why do you ask?"

"I just wondered why he doesn't seem to object that you are spending so much time with me since I am a Muslim. And tonight we are going to be with a Christian as well. I thought such associations are forbidden in Judaism, yet your aunt and uncle have welcomed me into their home. They treat me like a daughter. I thought Judaism was very strict on these issues."

"My aunt and uncle are not like many orthodox Jews. They are what I believe every Jew should be. At first I was really concerned about how they would react to our friendship. But I was amazed at how open they are. In the beginning my aunt cried a lot but she didn't really say anything. I don't know if she cried because she thought our friendship was wrong or because she thought that we might someday fall in love and it would be a very painful relationship. I think Uncle Samuel asked her to remain silent and let time answer the questions. My uncle even laughed that I would be worried about what he would think. He told me that this is an issue between HaShem and me with the counsel of my rabbi."

Aaron was silent for a moment as he reflected, then he continued. "If I ever told my uncle that I loved you and that I was going to marry you he would pause then ask if I am certain of my decision. He would drop everything to discuss it with me in detail. He would begin my telling me about my father and my mother and how they were righteous Jews. He would place his right hand on top of his left, on his desk, and lower his head for a few seconds with a look of sadness then he would look up and smile. He would tell me that I am a man of HaShem and that these are decisions that only I can make though counsel with a rabbi is not only suggested but required in such decisions. He would remind me of King Solomon and his relationships with women outside of Judaism and the consequences that it had for the people of Israel. Then he would provide other examples of such relationships, some with good results and some with bad, and he would talk about halacha and Rambam and the various views of those within Judaism. He would tell me that he believes that I should wait and allow HaShem time to provide an answer without violating halacha. Then he would say that he loves me and that Aunt Sarah loves me and that no matter what I decide to do, they will continue to love me as their own son."

"Wow," replied Al Zahra. "Your uncle reminds me of my father. If I told him that I was going to marry a Jew he would tell me much the same thing that your uncle would tell you but then he would elaborate. He would remind me of the hatred between the Jews and the Arabs and that this was foretold in the ancient prophecies. He would tell me of the serious consequences of such a decision and he would tell me that we live in Palestine and not in America. He would tell me that if I marry a Jew it could mean that the family would be harassed and possibly even imprisoned because he is a well known Muslim with wide reaching influences. He would then tell me that Islam has been influenced by evil men who violate the laws and the covenants set forth by Mohammad. He would remind me that Mohammad's objection to Judaism was only that Jews had failed to honor the requirements of leadership placed upon them by the Torah and the prophets and that Mohammad believed that in time, Jews will come to understand this failure when Mahdi to Muslims, and Moshiach to Jews, appears and explains it all. Then Jews will fulfill their obligations under the Torah and we will see the true Kingdom of A'lah or as you would say HaShem. He would say that many within Islam have used the teachings of Mohammad to subvert the truth and have falsely taught that he advocated the destruction of Jews. He did not. He advocated the reunion of Jews and Muslims in the Messianic era. My father would tell me that our family is righteous and is devoted to serving A'lah and that if it means that leaders within Islam are teaching false doctrine, the entire family would be ready to die for my decision to marry a Jew. My father is very wise and I think that my father should meet your uncle."

Aaron sat silently with his hands on the lower part of the steering wheel. He could not think of anything to say. Finally he leaned over to hug Al Zahra and said, "I love your family even though I have never met them."

Aaron proudly sported his Barcelino Alessandro as he walked into David's. When he removed the Alessandro his yarmulke continued to shield his head. "Aaron, this is Monica," said Al Zahra. "I know you have seen her around Barnes."

"Yes," I have," replied Aaron. "How are you Monica?"

"I am well," she replied. "I like your gangster hat. I haven't seen it in the school," she said with a laugh.

Aaron and Al Zahra both laughed. "You must be referring to my Borcelino. Yes, this is a popular hat among the Chassidic Jews of Chabad. It was made popular by the Lubavitcher Rebbe Menachem Schneerson. Although I am not Chabad I like the hat."

"It looks really good on you," replied Monica. "I also like the shirt you are wearing under the suit or sports jacket. But what are those little strings hanging down. It looks like you forgot to tie something." Monica suddenly looked embarrassed, "Oh Aaron, I am so sorry I must sound like an idiot. As Al Zahra can tell you I have an uncanny ability to put my foot in my mouth. Please don't be offended"

Aaron laughed again as he said, "It's okay. I understand that this is all new to you. We have plenty of time to learn of each other's cultures. Al Zahra said that you would like to learn a Jew's view of Christianity. I don't mind sharing with you but I have to tell you that Jews are forbidden from trying to convert others to Judaism."

"I understand that," replied Monica. The reason I would like to know is that there is a common belief among Christians that Jews rejected Christianity because they were "blind" or "ignorant" to the truth and could not recognize J'sus as the messiah when he came. Al Zahra tells me that it is far more complicated than that and that Judaism has thoroughly analyzed the issue of the messiah and reached its conclusions after a great deal of consideration. Is that true?"

"Yes, you will find that to be true," replied Aaron.

As they were being seated at the table Monica said, "I want to thank both of you for inviting me to dinner this evening. Aaron, I really appreciate your willingness to share your beliefs with me. I hope you don't mind."

Aaron replied, "Of course not, as long as you understand that the way of Judaism is not to tell others that they are in error. True Judaism recognizes that HaShem speaks to many people in different ways. For those who are not Jews, in the eyes of Judaism, the real issue is whether they comply with the noahide laws in a relationship with G-d."

"Al Zahra told me about the noahide laws. It seems that they are almost the Ten Commandments."

"Many of the Ten Commandments are contained within the noahide laws," said Aaron. "These were the laws that were given to people up until the time Moses gave the Torah to the Jews. Even so, the noahide laws remain in effect for non Jews. The 613 laws given to the Jews were only for the Jews. Non Jews are not required, or even permitted to try to follow them because if one follows one of them, he must follow all of them."

"I have also heard that the Ten Commandments and the seven noahide laws were contained in the Egyptian Book of the Dead and taught by the rulers of Egypt. Is that true?" asked Monica.

"Although the Torah speaks unfavorably of the ancient Egyptians it is important to remember that this had to do largely with their treatment of the Jews. Remember that it was Joseph who came to Egypt hundreds of years earlier and taught the ways of Avraham to the Egyptians. Certainly this teaching would have included not only the noahide laws but the secret teachings of Malchezzadik, the ancestor of Avraham and the King of Salem, which later became Jerusalem. These teachings would have been adopted by the Egyptian religious teachers and in fact, remember that not only did the descendants of Joseph include pharaohs of

Egypt but Joseph even married the daughter of the priest of the Egyptian sun god O'n. Also, the nursemaid of Moses was his own mother who most likely taught him many things of Judaism," explained Aaron.

"It is interesting that you say that the gentiles were not required to observe the 613 laws but only the seven noahide laws. This, I believe is a source of confusion for many Christians," said Monica. "Most Christians seem to believe that everyone was at one time required to follow all the laws of the Torah including the 613 laws until J'sus freed them from these laws. But you are saying that they were not."

"No they were not required to follow the 613 laws," said Aaron. "In that sense, if the message of J'sus was to the gentile, when he said that they did not have to follow the 613 laws then his message was true. However, whether the result of mistranslations or other reasons, many have tried to say that he came to free the Jews from the 613 commandments. According to Judaism this is clearly in error and would be heresy. We are told at Devarim 7:9, or what you call Deuteronomy 7:9, that HaShem is faithful and that He will keep his covenants with those who keep His commandments until a thousand generations. This referred to the 613 commandments. Whatever Christianity teaches, it cannot contradict the Torah because it is based upon Torah. Secondly, no book, whether the Qur'an or what Christians call the New Testament, can replace or supersede the Torah. Jews have no quarrel with noahide faiths and in fact, are commanded both in scripture and by the rabbis, to be respectful of other faiths. The problem for Jews arises when Christians, or Muslims or anyone else for that matter, tries to convert them from Judaism to that other religion. It is clearly forbidden for a Jew to turn from Judaism to another religion."

"You know," said Monica, "many Christian leaders have now said that Jews have a special covenant with G-d and that Christians should not try to convert them to Christianity. This seems consistent with what you are saying. But I have also heard that some Jews consider Christianity to be idol worship. Is that true?"

"Yes, this was the belief of the famous Rabbi Maimonides, better known as Rambam, and it is the belief of many today. The reason is that Christianity assigns the status of a deity to a man, namely J'sus, and says that he is part of a trinity. Neither the trinity nor any created thing including a man can ever be G-d, in Orthodox Judaism. I want to explain that there is much disagreement among Jews as to whether Christians can be noahides. Almost all orthodox Jews agree that for Jews the trinity is avodah zara (idolatry). However, a majority of Jews today, including many orthodox Jews, also believe that Christianity is a form of noahide worship for the gentile. In other words, while a Jew cannot follow Christianity and remain true to Orthodox Judaism, Christians are accepted by many Jews as noahides. As I said Rambam did not believe that they could be noahides. However, Rabbenu Tam, the grandson of the famous Rabbi Shlomo Yitzchaki better known as Rashi, taught that for gentiles the trinity could be accepted as a form of "shittuf." The concept of shittuf is that one makes an association or a connection to G-d through an intermediary but worships the one true G-d and not the intermediary. Rabbenu Tam had associations with many Christian businessmen of his day and based on his understanding of Christianity, as he learned it from them, concluded that most Christians do not worship J'sus the man but rather worship an abstract concept of the G-d of Judaism wherein J'sus serves as the intermediary. It would be entirely different if J'sus was a man alive and walking the earth but since he is not present in physical form, he can only be a concept and not a human being who is worshipped. Thus, while the Christian faith has many teachings that are outside of Judaism, many Jews believe that it is a legitimate form of noachide worship. One rabbi has even formed an organization called the International Fellowship of Christians and Jews, which brings Christians and Jews together for common interests. That organization is receiving a mixed reception by leaders in the Jewish community."

"That is fascinating," replied Monica.

"Aaron, can you explain why Jews do not believe that J'sus can be the promised messiah descended from King David whom Jews refer to as Moshiach ben David?" asked Al Zahra.

"Yes, I will if Monica wants to hear it. I don't want to discuss it if she would find it offensive," said Aaron.

"No, I would like to hear it," replied Monica. "I think it is really important for Christians to be tolerant of other faiths and to understand why they believe what they do."

"Ok, let's start with the idea of a messiah. In Judaism, unlike in Christianity, a messiah is not a G-d. In Judaism a messiah is simply a man who is anointed by HaShem to perform a specific task. In that respect, Moses was a messiah. David and Solomon were messiahs. Because Christianity has used the term messiah to refer to G-d, Jewish scholars almost exclusively use the Hebrew term Moshiach to refer to the final messiah who would come at an appointed time to fulfill the messianic tasks. The term Moshiach is derived from the term comforter and is a Hebrew pronunciation of the term messiah. If we examine the text that you call the "Old Testament," which we call the Tanakh, we will see that there is no writing, in the original Hebrew or a legitimate translation of the Hebrew text, which refers to the messiah as G-d. This would be heresy to a Jew."

Aaron paused to allow Monica an opportunity to reflect upon what had been said. Monica nodded her head indicating her understanding and Aaron continued.

"This is one of the primary problems that Jews have with Christianity. Can you find, anywhere in the Tanakh, your Old Testament, where we are told that the messiah would be G-d? Where then did that idea come from? Actually, Jews believe that it came from the pagan religions of the world. Going back to ancient Egypt there was the teaching that the pharaohs were descended from a god. The Greeks believed that various leaders were gods. Added to this, in pagan teaching, was the idea that the first of the man/gods was the son of a virgin and his father was a god. This teaching was all over the Middle East at the time J'sus came on the scene. Even more than that, there was a common teaching that the man/god was born of a virgin in a stable or a cave, lived his life, died at an early age then resurrected to complete his messianic mission. This teaching existed in many religions long before Christianity. When confronted with this information, the early Catholic Church responded by saying that those who propounded these early religions were actually having prophetic glimpses of the true messiah. Of course, Orthodox Judaism rejects this answer and maintains that Christianity simply adopted the pagan teachings in an effort to impress the leaders of Rome."

"You are saying that the idea of a virgin birth, the death and the resurrection were not presented for the first time in Christianity? They were actually taught in dozens of religions before Christianity?" asked Monica.

"Yes, that is correct," replied Aaron. "You will find these teachings in the ancient Egyptian religions, the Greek religions, the Roman religions and the religions of various pagan people since the beginning of time. The Israelites considered this heresy and Jews believe that it is because of the infiltration of these ideas into Israel that the Israelites were driven into exile where they remain to this day."

"But I understand that the Old Testament, or the Tanakh as the Jews call it, says that the Messiah would be born of a virgin. Isn't that correct?"

"Actually no," replied Aaron. "The passage you are probably referring to is Isaiah 7:14 which is interpreted by Christians to state that a virgin will give birth to the messiah. In the Christian Bible, and specifically at Matthew 1:22-23, reliance is placed upon this passage to show that J'sus, who was claimed to be born of a virgin, is the fulfillment of this passage from Isaiah. However, the interpretation cited in Matthew was based upon the Greek translation of Isaiah wherein the word parthenos is used to describe the mother of the messiah. The word parthenos indeed means virgin. But the problem is that the Tanakh was not written in Greek. It was written in Hebrew and the Hebrew term in this passage is alma which simply means a young woman. Moreover, Jews do not believe that this passage even refers to the messiah. But assuming for the sake of argument that it does then Isaiah simply says that the messiah would be born of a young woman not that he would be born of a virgin. Again, in Judaism the idea that the messiah would be born of a virgin is just another restatement of the pagan mystery religions that people tried to push on them throughout the centuries. This is the reason so many Jews struggle so severely with Christianity even more so than Islam."

"But let's move on. What are we told about the messiah according to the Tanakh? First, Jews know that he must be a patrilineal descendant of King David. How do we know that? Well for one thing, inheritance rights and kingship always passed from father to son in ancient Israel. They did not pass from father to daughter and kingship was an inherited position. Secondly, we are told in several passages in the Tanakh that the messiah would be of the seed of King David and that the line would pass through David's son Solomon.

Aaron paused briefly then continued, "It is important to see that the word zera or seed of David is used in the verses that address this. As you know, the seed of a man is his Y chromosome whereas the seed of a woman is her X chromosome. A man's Y chromosome cannot pass through a woman. It can only pass through a man. In other words, a woman cannot pass on male sperm or seed or Y DNA. This means that any woman in the chain breaks the chain and her son or other heirs cannot be the final messiah who is descended from David. We are given the genealogy of Mary in Luke and we are given the genealogy of Joseph in Matthew. The genealogy of Mary goes through Nathan and not Solomon and thus, this cannot be the line from King David from which the messiah would come. In fact, that line passes through Mary who was a woman and so it cannot be the seed of David. In contrast, the genealogy in Matthew does not pass through Joseph though it does pass through Solomon. However, Christians assert that Joseph was not his father but that G-d was his father, and thus this genealogy is irrelevant since it is not the genealogy of J'sus."

"To state it in purely biological terms, think of it this way. Every human being inherits 23 chromosomes from each of his/her parents for a total of 46 chromosomes. 44 of these chromosomes called autosomes are non-sex chromosomes and are identical in men and women. However, the sex chromosomes, or the seed, differ between men and women. Women inherit two X chromosomes whereas men inherit one Y chromosome from his father and one X chromosome from his mother."

"It is because of this inheritance that we are able to determine the identity of ancestors 100's of generations passed. It works as follows: A man passes on the Y-DNA he received from his father and his father's father etc all the way back to the first man. This is the man's "seed" which is one of the definitions of zera. In contrast, a woman passes on her mother's X chromosome. A woman cannot pass on the Y-DNA. In fact, she cannot even receive it. However, we can trace a woman's DNA all the way back to the first woman through her X chromosome."

"Let me explain how this relates to the genealogy of J'sus. Once again, here is how the process works biologically. As I mentioned earlier there are 22 autosomes (non-sex chromosomes) from each parent and one sex chromosome from each parent. The male gametes contain either an X or a Y chromosome. The female gametes contain only the X chromosome because a woman cannot produce male "seed." If the male gamete contains a Y chromosome, which fertilizes the female gamete (X chromosome) then the child will be male. If it contains an X chromosome which fertilizes the female gamete, then the child will be female. Since only an X chromosome in the male gamete will produce a female, and a Y chromosome in the male gamete always produces a male, it is impossible for a female to ever carry a Y chromosome. Hence, Mary could not pass on the seed (Y-chromosome) of King David to J'sus. It was a physical impossibility. And while J'sus carried his mother's X chromosome (sex chromosome) had he married and produced children that chromosome would not have gone on to his child because it would have been replaced by his wife's X-chromosome even though his male descendants would have carried his Y-chromosome. This is today regarded by many Jewish scientists as the greatest evidence supporting the proposition that J'sus did not carry the "seed" of King David and thus cannot have been Moshiach ben David."

"Let me make sure I understand what you are saying," said Monica. "You are saying that Old Testament scriptures say that the messiah must be a male line descendant of King David through his son Solomon with no woman breaking the chain. It is clear from the scriptures that it says that the messiah would descend from Solomon and Christians claim that J'sus was descended from Nathan, Solomon's brother, but not from Solomon since Joseph, who was descended from Solomon, was not his father. G-d was his father. Therefore, what you are saying is that according to Orthodox Judaism the mere fact that he was not descended from Solomon would alone preclude J'sus from being the messiah from the line of David. Then, if you add the fact that J'sus was not a male line descendant of either Nathan or Solomon, but only a descendant of Nathan through his mother, then he would seem to be precluded completely from being the messiah. So, if he wasn't the messiah, who was he?"

Aaron continued, "There is quite a bit of discussion among Jews of who he was. Some have asked if he was possibly Moshiach ben Joseph, referenced in pre-Christian Jewish writings to refer to a religious messiah, who was the son of a man named Joseph who would die early in his life and then be resurrected. However, this view is not widely accepted in Judaism. Most Jews simply say he is not relevant to Judaism even though he was important to the gentile. Some say that he and his friends tried to restore the Jewish monarchy in the bloodline of Nathan but this was doomed to failure since he was not descended from Solomon. Some say that he is actually an evil false prophet described in Daniel who would lead the world astray. For most of us, our tolerance of other religions doesn't require that we identify him as any form of false prophet or anything of that nature. Rambam said that in some respects he will have served the world well because he will have prepared everyone for the concept of a messiah so that when the real messiah comes, the world will understand and accept him. Now interestingly, there is a book in what you call the New Testament called Revelation that identifies a person called the antichrist who in many respects is similar to what Judaism teaches will be the messiah except his intentions are evil. Many Jewish scholars believe that the Book of Revelation was written specifically to discredit any potential messiah who would come after Jesus and reveal that Jesus was not the Moshiach ben David."

"But some in Christianity would say that because G-d was the father of J'sus that was even better than being descended from King Solomon and that obviated the need to descend through Solomon," said Monica.

"That is irrelevant," replied Aaron. "In the Tanakh we are given extremely specific instructions concerning how to identify the messiah. One of those instructions was that he would be a male line descendant of King Solomon. If a potential candidate is not a descendant of King Solomon, then he is not Moshiach ben David, period. We were told repeatedly that not one word can change in terms of these commandments and prophecies."

Monica said, "I have never heard anything like this before at any time in my life and my father is a minister. Why are not Christians aware of these issues?"

"We have only just begun looking at the issues," said Aaron. "The reasons Christians are not aware of these issues is that Jews were not permitted to address these issues to Christians until the time of the arrival of Moshiach ben David. Remember earlier I said that Jews are prohibited from trying to convert others to Judaism?"

Monica asked, "You said that Jews are not supposed to disclose this information until the arrival of the final messiah. But you are telling me. Why?"

"Because you asked," replied Aaron with a smile.

"Okay, let me ask you this," said Monica. "What are Messianic Jews?"

"Messianic Jews are Jews who do believe that J'sus was the messiah," replied Aaron.

"So are they still Jews or are they now Christians," asked Al Zahra.

"Well they are still Jews but according to Orthodox Judaism they are not following true Judaism," replied Aaron. "They don't stop being Jews because they believe J'sus was the messiah, but they do not fit within the definition of orthodox, conservative or even reformed Judaism. They observe Jewish traditions and hold traditional style services, but they insert J'sus into their faith as the messiah."

"So is that bad," asked Monica.

"As long as they don't worship J'sus as a deity it probably does not violate any law of Judaism. There is no law against believing that someone is the messiah. Many people in Chabad believe that the Lubavitchar Rebbe was the messiah. While I do not see this belief as correct, I don't believe it violates halacha. If they start saying he is G-d then they would be outside of acceptable Judaism and that would be idol worship because Jews are expressly forbidden from worshipping any physical thing. I suppose it would be the same with Messianic Jews. If they don't consider J'sus to be G-d then they are probably not violating any laws of Judaism."

"Okay, let's take a look at the prophecies concerning what the messiah will do," continued Aaron. "By looking at the prophecies about the final messiah we can see if they have been fulfilled and if they have not, then Jews would say that Moshiach ben David has not yet come. We are told many things in the scripture to allow us to identify the final messiah."

"Like what?" asked Monica.

"For one thing, we are told at Isaiah 2:3, he will be a great political leader and his counsel will be sought by people from around the world. And we are told in Daniel 7:14 that he will be given a kingdom that will never be destroyed or taken away from him.

The problem is that J'sus was never given a kingdom and he never ruled over any nation. Christians answer this by saying that he was given a spiritual kingdom in heaven. But that is not what the passages tell us…' Jews believe that to say that this refers to a spiritual kingship is basic scripture twisting. Given that kind of analysis one can get scripture to say anything one wants it to say."

"We are told at Isaiah 2:4 that Moshiach will bring worldwide peace and will bring an end to wars. J'sus did not bring world peace. In fact, there have been more wars, death and destruction since his arrival than at any time in history. So this prophecy was not fulfilled either."

"We are told in Ezekiel 37:26-28 and elsewhere that Moshiach will build, or cause to be built, the temple in Jerusalem which will remain there forever. Similar statements are made at Isaiah 33:20 and in Ezekiel chapters 40-48. J'sus did not build the third temple and he didn't build the second temple. The second temple was built long before his arrival and it was destroyed in CE 70, nearly 37 years after his death. Today the third temple is not yet built so this hasn't happened yet. As you can see, prophecy was not fulfilled by J'sus."

"In Isaiah 11:12 we are told that Moshiach will gather the Jews from the far corners of the world and bring them back to Israel. Similar statements are made at Isaiah 43:5-6; Jeremiah 16:15 and elsewhere. While after 1948 there has been an influx of Jews into Israel, nothing like this happened at the time of J'sus. This tells us that we are now ready for Moshiach, not 2000 years ago. There was no influx of Jews into Israel until now."

"At Ezekiel 37:22 we are told that Moshiach will be the king over all Israel. J'sus was never made king over all of Israel and Israel was never united into a single nation. Some called J'sus King of Israel but it was never an official title of any kind and he never ruled in any capacity. In fact, he was put to death for trying. Thus, this prophecy was not fulfilled by J'sus."

"We are told in Isaiah 26:19 that at the time of Moshiach the righteous will rise from the dead. This is known as the resurrection. Similar statements were made in Ezekiel 37:12-13 and Daniel 12:2. Nothing like this occurred during the time of J'sus so we have yet another unfulfilled prophecy."

"In Isaiah 11:9 we are told that there will be a universal knowledge of G-d and that there will be no more wars and destruction. Similar statements were made at Jeremiah 31:33 and Zechariah 14:9. Of course, Israel has had numerous wars with her neighbors. Today her mountains are anything but safe and there is almost no knowledge of G-d throughout the world. Today the world is full of false religions and beliefs contrary to the teachings of HaShem."

Monica and Al Zahra sat silently looking at the table for a few minutes. Finally, Monica said, "Aaron you know, don't you, that Christians believe that J'sus will return and fulfill all of the prophecies that were not fulfilled the first time he was here? How do Jews respond to that?"

Aaron smiled and said, "Ah yes, the second bite at the apple theory. You know Monica there is not one passage in the entire Tanakh, again what you would call the Old Testament, which even remotely suggests that the messiah would come, begin his work, die then return and complete what he was unable to complete the first time he was here. In fact, if he fails to complete the tasks for which he came, the first time he is here, including the fulfillment of all the messianic prophecies, then he cannot be the messiah. That is why most Jews do not believe that Lubavitcher Rebbe was Moshiach. One could conclude that anyone is the messiah based upon the absurd idea that any failed messiah can come back for a second bite at the apple to complete where he failed the first time around. By that standard, George Washington and John F. Kennedy could be the messiah. Do you know where the second bite at the apple theory came from?"

"I don't know," replied Monica. "Where did it come from?"

"Do you remember our discussion earlier about the pagan mystery religions? What were some of the common features of the mystery religions?" asked Aaron.

"The two things that stand out are virgin birth and the resurrection of the man/god after which he performs his messianic tasks," replied Monica. "So you are saying that the idea of a second bite at the apple came from the theories about the resurrection of a god/man after which he would complete the tasks he started before he died."

"That's right," replied Aaron. "The common theme of the pagan mystery religions is that after the death of the messiah god/man he would resurrect and return and finish the messianic tasks that he started before he died."

"You know though," said Monica, "Christianity doesn't teach that J'sus failed but rather that he willfully forfeited his life as atonement for sins which abolished the need for an animal sacrifice. So in that respect it wouldn't really be a second bite at the apple, it would be a fulfillment of the original mission."

Aaron didn't say anything further. He just looked at Monica with a smile. She looked at him and laughed, "What? Why are you looking at me like that?" He did not reply.

As Aaron paid the check Monica said, "Aaron, this has been a very interesting conversation. I cannot describe my amazement at the things you told me. I am going to have to think about this for a long time and do some extensive research. I will also need to talk to my dad about it. Thank you so much for sharing with me. You have opened my eyes to a lot of things that need to be addressed in Christianity and you have given me a lot to think about."

"If you do the research you will find that what I am telling you is true," said Aaron.

"I think it is very important that Christians learn this information," said Monica. "I would really like to hear what leading Christian scholars would say about these things. Don't you think it would be really good if Christians and Jews got together to discuss these issues. I can tell you that my eyes are opened to many things after talking to you. I can tell you that most Christians think that Jews do not accept J'sus as the messiah because they are "blind" and "ignorant" and that they missed all the signs of the messiah when J'sus came. Our discussion makes it clear that is not the case at all. Judaism has put a great deal of thought and research into this issue and they have reasons for their positions. I am not saying that I have been persuaded that what you told me is true. What I am saying is that Judaism does not reject J'sus out of ignorance as most Christians believe."

"Actually, leading Christian scholars and Messianic Jews debate Jewish rabbis on these issues all the time. Some of them are recorded and broadcast on various radio stations. You would probably find these discussions very interesting.

I will see if I can find a podcast of one of the debates and will let you know in advance," replied Aaron.

"That is wonderful Aaron," said Al Zahra. "I think it is great that people of different faiths can engage in these kinds of discussions. Wasn't it the famous philosopher John Stuart Mill who said that it is important for people to discuss their views with those of opposing views because it can help them understand their own views better and in some cases it might show them that their views are incorrect? I think it is that way with religion. I just wish I were better prepared to respond to you tonight. These are new issues for me."

As they left David's Monica said again, "Aaron, I don't know what to say. I have never heard anything like this before. I need to do the research and really think about everything you have said. I really need some time to think it through." Monica paused for a moment then said, "I have an idea. It is still early, why don't both of you come over to my apartment and we can watch a DVD. I rented some that just came out. I am sure one of them would be good."

"What do you think, Al Zahra? Do you want to see a DVD?" asked Aaron.

"Actually, that might be fun," said Al Zahra.

"Ok, then follow me to my apartment," said Monica. "If I lose you I will pull over and wait for you. You have my cell number in case you get lost," she said as she got into her Toyota.

As they drove behind Monica down Forsyth Al Zahra asked, "Do you like Monica, Aaron?"

"Yes, she seems like a very nice person," Aaron replied.

"I thought you would like her," said Al Zahra as she put her left hand on Aaron's right hand that was resting on the shifter.

When they arrived at the apartment Monica invited them to sit on the couch as she presented several DVD's from which they could select. Aaron said "this one looks good" as he pointed at one of them.

"I think so too," said Al Zahra. "What do you think Monica?"

"It looks good to me too," she said as she put it in the DVD player then sat on the couch next to Aaron and passed a bowl of popcorn. "Oh, I almost forgot. I just got a bottle of Mondavi for my birthday. Would you like some?

"Oh, you know Muslims don't drink alcohol," said Al Zahra. "But I appreciate the offer."

"Oh, I didn't know that. How about you Aaron?" she said.

"Oh, no thank you," said Aaron. "I am fine."

"As Aaron sat on the couch, with Monica to his left and Al Zahra to his right, Monica suddenly laughed, "Look at you Aaron, you look like quite the ladies' man here."

"Yeah you do," laughed Al Zahra. "What are you pulling off anyway? I think you are up to no good."

"Hey, I'm not doing anything," laughed Aaron. "I think you two are up to something. You are the ones who sat up this date. I hope you don't think I'm easy," he said with a feigned expression of terror.

Later that evening, as the second DVD ended, Monica said, "Wow, I just realized it is 2:30 in the morning. You two are probably too tired to drive home tonight. Why don't you spend the night? I have a spare bedroom. Monica you can use it if you like and Aaron you can use the couch, or the other way around if you prefer. Heck I don't care, you can do whatever you like," she said with a laugh.

"Now I am really beginning to think you girls are up to something," laughed Aaron. "I can use the couch. I don't mind. Do you want to stay here tonight Al Zahra?"

"Actually, that would be fun," Al Zahra replied. "We can get up in the morning and have a nice breakfast."

"It's a deal then," said Monica. "There is a shower in the bathroom in the hall by the bedroom you can use."

As Aaron turned off the light next to the couch and lay down he thought of the conversation he had that evening with Monica. He also thought to himself how interesting it was that he had found this friendship with these two extremely beautiful women both of whom are forbidden desires. "What does HaShem have in store for me," he thought to himself with a smile.

As he was falling asleep on the couch Aaron was awakened by a gentle touch of a hand on his face. In the darkness he could make out Al Zahra's features as she knelt on the floor beside the couch. "Aaron," she said, "do you mind if I sit with you for awhile. I am feeling some strange warm emotions tonight."

"You haven't even been drinking," said Aaron with a smile. "What is prompting this?"

"I don't know she said as she rested her head on his chest. I just want to be close to you."

"Well don't sit on the floor. You can lie on the couch with me if you promise to behave," he said.

"I thought you would never ask," replied Al Zahra as she climbed on the couch. Lying on her side facing him, she put her arm across Aaron's chest and her head on his shoulder. Aaron put his arm under her back to give her support. They were silent for a little while then Aaron felt Al Zahra kiss him on the cheek.

"Aaron, you know that I would not resist you if you wanted to be with me don't you?"

"Yes, I know that," Aaron replied. "But we agreed that it would not be good for us. For one thing, once we cross that line there is no going back. We always knew that we couldn't be together romantically but we chose this path of friendship anyway. We both know that we can't give in to this emotion and desire. Believe me I want to," said Aaron, "but it would be a mistake."

"I am ready to give in to it and forget everything else," she said.

Aaron held her close and said, "I know that is what you want but we agreed that we wouldn't do this. Now if you don't behave I am going to give you into a cold shower."

"Well that's a start," she giggled.

Aaron laughed as he gave her a gentle embrace.

Al Zahra nestled closer to Aaron then they both drifted gently into slumber. The next morning they were awakened by the laugh of Monica who had just entered the living room and said, "What are you two doing out here? There is another room for that."

"Oh I tried to get him in there all night but it was pointless. I thought maybe you could help me this morning," she said with a laugh.

"Well I suppose we could tag team him," laughed Monica.

"Oh, this is what I get for hanging out with a couple of non kosher super hot girls," laughed Aaron as he sat up on the couch rubbing the sleep out of his eyes. "Now I know why you girls are forbidden to Jews."

"Just for that…," said Al Zahra as she hit him in the head with a pillow.

"Yeah," said Monica as she ran over and jumped on the couch in front of Aaron and began tickling him.

"Are you ticklish, Mr. Will Power of Steel?" said Al Zahra as she jumped on top of Aaron and began tickling him as well. Aaron pretended to resist the tickling of both girls who were giggling hysterically. After about two minutes of feigned resistance he suddenly put one arm around each of them and rolled onto the floor. He then said, "This is what Mr. Will Power of Steel can do," as he held both of them down on the floor one with each hand while tickling each of them with the hand that was holding each one to the floor.

Monica looked at Al Zahra who looked back at her as they lay on the floor laughing. "He is really strong," she said. Finally, after several minutes of frolicking, Aaron sat on the floor and they all sat up laughing.

Then Monica said, "I thought of something last night. A Muslim a Christian and a Jew walk into a bar. The bartender looks up and asks, 'what is this some kind of joke.'"

"Ok, I have one," laughed Aaron.

"Becky, who belonged to a synagogue group devoted to visiting and helping the sick members of her congregation, was out making her rounds visiting homebound patients when she ran out of gas. As luck would have it a gas station was just a block away. She walked to the station to borrow a gas can and buy some gas. The attendant told her the only gas can he owned had been loaned out but she could wait until it was returned."

"Since Becky was on the way to see another patient and behind schedule she decided not to wait and walked back to her car. She looked for something in her car that she could fill with gas and spotted the bedpan she always had handy for needy patients. Always resourceful she carried the bedpan to the station, filled it with gas, and carried the full bedpan back to her car which was decorated with many Hebrew decals and bumper stickers."

"As she was pouring the gas into her tank, two men watched from across the street. One of them turned to the other and said, 'If it starts, I'm turning Jewish.'"

"You nut," laughed Al Zahra. "Now I have one. Family hug," she said as she put one arm around Aaron and one arm around Monica then pulled them close to her. As they hugged each other Monica asked, "Does this mean I am part of the family now?"

"You can't get out of it," replied Al Zahra. "Right, Aaron?"

"Absolutely," laughed Aaron. "You are in."

VII

Five months had passed since the dinner at David's where Aaron and Al Zahra met Monica. "Hey guys." said Aaron as he, Al Zahra and Monica walked past several third year medical students who responded with pleasantries. Proceeding through the corridors of Barnes Jewish Hospital, with Al Zahra to the left and Monica to the right, the three joked and laughed as they walked.

"Can you believe that," said Roger McMahon. "During his entire first year he ran around the medical school with Al Zahra, one of the two most beautiful girls on campus. Now, he has Monica too, the other of the two most beautiful girls in this school. How does he do it?"

"I don't know but I am going to become a Jew," laughed Larry Evans.

"Moshe is a Jew but he doesn't have the two most beautiful women in medical school hanging on his arms," replied Roger.

"Yeah but Moshe is ugly," replied Larry with a laugh. "I'm joking Moshe."

"Hey," said Moshe as he threw a gum wrapper at Larry with a laugh. "Actually, his success with women isn't just from being a Jew I or would have a couple of girls too. I mean good grief he looks like a movie star."

As Aaron, Monica and Al Zahra approached the cafeteria, Monica said, "I have something I need to tell both of you."

"What is it?" asked Al Zahra.

"Well, it goes back to the night we had dinner at David's. I haven't mentioned it before but that night really caused me to start thinking about a lot of things. I had never heard anything like you told me that night Aaron. I went home and told my father everything you said. He was just as amazed as I was. If you recall, I had asked if we could meet so that I could respond to everything you said."

"I recall that," replied Aaron.

"The reality is, after many hours of research and thought, I can't really respond to much of anything that you said. It is as if you already answered the questions I would have asked if I had understood what you were going to tell me," she said, "My world has opened up in many new ways since we spoke. I want to share that with both of you," continued Monica.

"What do you want to tell us," asked Al Zahra. "You are building up to something."

"Well, don't worry, I am not going to convert to Judaism," she said, "but I am rethinking much of what I previously believed. I have begun studying the ancient Jewish writings and it is giving me a new depth of understanding that I didn't have before. All I can say is that it is a wonderful experience. You have opened my eyes to many things Aaron that will allow me to understand my own faith much more deeply."

"But there is more," Monica continued. "Instead of going to Brazil, I have also decided to go to Palestine to work with the Red Cross through the Red Crescent, once I complete my residency. That way I can be close to you two. Aaron, if you get the residency you would like you will be at Hadassah-Hebrew University Medical Center in Jerusalem. You plan to stay in Israel after that and Al Zahra, you will be doing your residency at Al Shifa Hospital in Damascus. I will do my residence here if I am accepted. Then I will come to where you both are. We will be within driving distance of one another. This divine friendship will continue even after we graduate."

Aaron and Al Zahra were both amazed. "That is fantastic," said Aaron. "But we haven't even discussed our beliefs since that night at David's. I had no idea that you were even impressed by anything I said." Aaron paused momentarily then continued, "If you really do this we will be close enough that we can all get together on weekends. That would be really awesome."

"I am happy for you," said Al Zahra, with a forced smile, "but are you sure you would want to live in Palestine. It is nothing like here. In fact, it might even be dangerous for a Christian." Her thoughts were directed to the likelihood that Aaron and Monica would somehow become romantically involved and that could bring an end to her close friendship with Aaron. Her heart sank and she felt a knot it the pit of her stomach. "Maybe I am being paranoid but I already lost him once," she thought.

"That would be incredible," said Aaron.

"I am devoting my life to missionary work. It really doesn't matter if I am in Brazil or Palestine," Monica said looking at Al Zahra. "Would it bother you Al if I came to Palestine?" she asked. "I know that you and Aaron have been very close for a long time even though you aren't really romantic. But I don't want to be in the way, and I would never intentionally do anything to hurt either of you. You are the two best friends I have ever had and I love both of you very much. Would it bother you if I came to where you are?"

Al Zahra looked at the ground for a moment then said, "It wouldn't bother me. I think it would be wonderful. Remember, I am Muslim and Aaron is a Jew. Aaron and I can never be together. I will always love both of you no matter what. My only request is that if the two of you somehow connect in Israel and lose track of me, you will keep me close in your hearts and in your mind. If you do that I will be okay. Don't get me wrong, it would hurt a little if the two of you ever become romantically involved. But if you did, then I would wish the best for both of you."

"Wait a minute," said Monica. "I am not talking about Aaron and I becoming romantically involved. I am talking about a continuation of the friendship we have now."

"What are you thinking, Al?" asked Aaron. "She isn't talking about a romance. Where did all that come from?"

"I don't know," replied Al Zahra. "I guess I am just thinking out loud. I don't ever want to be a third wheel."

"Do you believe this nut?" asked Monica. "Al, I think you are losing it."

Al Zahra smiled, "I don't know. I just feel something inside. Anyhow, I have to run. I need to study for my final. I will talk to you tomorrow."

"Okay, Al Zahra," said Aaron. "I will call you in the morning."

Monica took a hold of Al Zahra's shoulders. Al Zahra looked to the side avoiding eye contact. Monica took her face in both her hands and forced her to look into her eyes. She whispered so Aaron couldn't hear, "Al Zahra, I love you. I will never hurt you okay?" She could see a tear forming in Al Zahra's eye.

"Okay," whispered Al Zahra. "My life has not been easy so far, but I have no right to stop you from being with him if it happens for you."

"I can't be with him either," Monica whispered. "I am a Christian and he is a Jew."

"I know, but I just thought I have detected something in the conversations lately. Maybe I am just being paranoid," replied Al Zahra.

"Alright you two, what is going on?" asked Aaron.

"Oh, nothing," replied Monica. "Just girl talk."

"Good night," said Al Zahra as she turned and walked to her car.

"Good night," replied Monica. "Don't worry Al. Everything will be alright."

The next day Monica and Al Zahra sat on a bench in Forest Park as they talked. They would often meet while Aaron was in class and talk about many matters such as their families and their plans after graduation.

"I think it would be a good idea for you to visit Palestine with me before deciding that is where you want to go," said Al Zahra. "The extreme Muslims do not look favorably upon Christians. They rank only slightly better than Jews in the eyes of many Muslims. It would not be a life of convenience."

"I understand that," replied Monica. "But like I said last night, I am devoting my life to G-d's work. I am willing to take whatever that brings to me. Just out of curiosity, if Palestine is so bad, why do you stay there? Your family is a prominent family of the Middle East and you are distant cousins of the king of Jordan. Why don't you leave Palestine and move to Egypt, Saudi Arabia or Jordan?"

"It is a long story," replied Al Zahra, "but the short version is that our family belongs in Israel according to our father. Our family lived in Jerusalem long before it ever became known as Israel. We have been there for thousands of years. We moved into the area that is today known as the Gaza Strip about two hundred years ago, because my ancestors had a beautiful estate on the beach. It was destroyed during the conflicts in the 1940's when the Jews began immigrating to Israel and the Arabs began to leave. We thought that we would only be in the Gaza Strip temporarily but it has turned out to be a half of a century already.

My father says we must stay there because it will be the center of the world when we are in the messianic era and we need to be there when that happens."

"Don't you think that there would be a place for me in Palestine?" asked Monica.

"If you try to convert people to Christianity it would be extremely dangerous," replied Al Zahra.

"I wouldn't try to convert people," Monica replied. "I would just help them with medical care and if they see the love of G-d in my actions and in my words, then I will have done what I am supposed to do."

"It is still a very dangerous thing you are proposing," said Al Zahra. "I am going home for a short break at the end of the second year, why don't you come with me. We can fly in through Lebanon then we can drive over and see Aaron in Jerusalem. He is going to stay for several weeks with a rabbi and his family. My parents would like you."

"Actually, that might be a good idea," replied Monica. "Let me check with my family and see if they are ok with the idea."

"Okay, then," replied Al Zahra.

It was the third week of May, 2003. Al Zahra, Monica and Aaron were finishing their second year of medical school. Aaron had made arrangements to visit a Chassidic rabbi in Jerusalem whom he had met at Washington University several years earlier while Al Zahra and Monica were traveling to Palestine to stay with Al Zahra's family for two weeks. Al Zahra and Monica arrived at the Gaza International Airport via Lebanon. The Abduls, who spoke English fluently, were very polite and kind to Monica. Even Al Zahra's 23 year old brother Monsoor came to the airport to meet Monica. Al Zahra had told him of Monica's beauty and great personality. The intrigue of meeting a beautiful

American woman overpowered his desire to appear disinterested in a female houseguest as protocol would dictate. As Al Zahra and Monica exited the gate at the airport Dr. Abdul hugged Al Zahra then turned to Monica and said, "You must be Monica. Al Zahra has told us so much about you. Welcome to Palestine."

Al Zahra's mother, in traditional clothing, extended her hand to Monica and said, "I am Fadilah, Al Zahra's mother. It is good to meet you. This is Monsoor," she said as she pulled Monsoor forward to meet Monica. "Have you eaten? We can stop somewhere if you are hungry."

"We ate on the plane," said Al Zahra. "Are you hungry?"

"No," replied Fadilah. "We ate as well."

After exchanging pleasantries they walked to the vehicle that was in the parking lot and loaded the bags into the trunk. As they drove back to the southern portion of the Gaza Strip, Monica noticed the traditional clothing of the women.

"When you go out it is probably wise to wear the traditional clothing," said Fadilah. "Some of the people here have gotten quite hostile over this issue. There have been a number of beatings of women for wearing western style clothing."

"Why is that happening?" asked Al Zahra.

"I suppose it is just changing times," replied Fadilah.

That evening they enjoyed a traditional meal much to Monica's delight. "The food is phenomenal," she said. "Fadilah, you are a wonderful cook."

"Thank you so much. I was so worried that you might not like it. Why don't we retire into the living room where it is more comfortable," said Fadilah as she began to clear the dishes.

As they sat in the living room Monica read a local newspaper noticing the anti Israel rhetoric that seemed to appear on every page.

"Al Zahra said that you are thinking about moving to Palestine when you finish your residency," said Dr. Abdul.

"My goal is to use my medical training where it is the most needed," she replied. "I understand that doctors are in short supply here in Palestine."

"Yes, that is true," replied Dr. Abdul. "I suppose there are many reasons for that. I think though, that most just want to get out to the world where they can enjoy the niceties of life. Many go to great medical schools in America or Europe and they don't come back."

Dr. Abdul paused for a few seconds then said, "Monica, life in Palestine is not easy. I have tried to convince Al Zahra that she shouldn't come back to Palestine when she finishes medical school but she won't listen. She believes this is where A'lah wants her. I can't argue with that if it is what she believes. What about you Monica? Why would you come to Palestine?"

"Well," replied Monica. "I think at first it was largely to be with Al Zahra," she said attempting to avoid any reference to Aaron. "But over time I have begun to think that this would be an excellent place for me to serve people who are in need, which is what I have always felt is my mission."

"You know that life is very hard here. It can even be dangerous," said Dr. Abdul. "Are you sure this is something you want to do?"

"Yes, this is what I believe G-d is calling me to do," she replied. Then she asked, "Why is there so much division between the Muslims and the Jews and why do so many Muslim people support terrorism?"

"Actually, most Muslim people do not support terrorism but the reason for the hatred among those who do requires that I tell a very long story," replied Dr. Abdul. "It is hard to say that it is totally the fault of either one side or the other. It goes back to the time of Avraham when the descendants of Ishmael went their way and the descendants of Isaac went their way. As you know they where both sons of Avraham. The Jews have maintained that the covenant of Avraham was given to them exclusively and not to the descendants of Ishmael. Muslims believe that a covenant was given to Jews but another covenant was given to the descendants of Ishmael. Muslims believe that the problem is that many Jews also believe that as a result of the covenant with the descendants of Isaac, Muslims were reduced to an inferior status in the eyes of G-d. But in taking this position, I believe those Jews violate the mandates of their own Tanakh"

"You know the Tanakh?" asked Monica in amazement.

"Sure," laughed Dr. Abdul. "I read it every day."

"I am really confused," said Monica. "I thought that Muslims didn't read the Tanakh and I thought that Muslims hate the Jews."

"Those you are speaking of have lost the ways of Mohammed. They have given up the truth for the confusion they have generated in their own minds because of the fanatical teachings," said Dr. Abdul. "According to the Qur'an the Jews are not the enemy. They are the brother of Ishmael."

"What are you referring to in the Qur'an that would cause you to say that," asked Monica in interest.

"There are many passages. Take for example Qur'an 5:23 where we are told that G-d encouraged the Jews to enter the promise land of Israel and stated that the land belongs to the Jews.

"Then why do some Muslims say that Israel should be driven into the sea and all Jews killed?" asked Monica.

"Because they have listened to the fanatical clerics and have fallen away from the true teachings of Mohammed. You see," continued Dr. Abdul, "the majority of people of Islam are peaceful. Unfortunately, with the peaceful personality also comes a peaceful nature. Those who engage in acts of terrorism are the fanatics who use force to push their agenda which is the execution of everyone except the Muslim including not only Jews but Christians as well. But this is in direct violation of the teachings of the Qur'an."

"Why is there so much hatred of Jews specifically in Palestine?" asked Al Zahra.

"It wasn't always that way," replied Dr. Abdul. "My father remembered what happened when he was a boy and he told me many times. The problem was a combination of interference by Britain who made a very bad decision for a reason unknown to the Arabs here at the time. The trouble began in large part with Grand Mufti Muhammed Amin al-Huseini. He was born in the 1890's. Even as a boy he spoke of killing all Jews in Palestine. Most Arabs wanted to live with the Jews in peace. Many were pleased that they were immigrating into Palestine because they believed it would enrich the culture and open opportunities for commerce. But Muhammed Amin al-Huseini wanted none of it. He was the son of the Mufti of Jerusalem who was a member of one of the most powerful families of Palestine. Muhammed Amin al-Huseini studied at al-Azhar University in Cairo and the Istanbul School of Administration. He quickly became known as a fanatic whose instructions were to slaughter all Jews. One of his first actions was an attack on Jews who were praying at the Western Wall. The Palestinian High Commissioner from Britain, was heavily influenced by anti-Zionists in Britain and he appointed Muhammed Amin al-Huseini as the Grand Mufti of Jerusalem in 1922 despite his known hatred and violence toward Jews. As time passed the Grand Mufti became extremely powerful. He issued an edict called "Izbah Al-Yahud" which means "slaughter the Jews." But it was even worse for Arabs who would not support his plan. They were tortured and killed by the hundreds of thousands until there was no one left who opposed the Mufti except those like my family who remained silent for their own safety. With the support of Britain, Muhammed Amin al-Huseini was simply too powerful for anyone to oppose."

"So, you are saying anti-Zionists in Britain are largely to blame for putting Muhammed Amin al-Huseini in power which in turn caused the problem we have today," asked Monica.

"In large part yes, but it is even worse. In April of 1936 six very powerful Arab men formed an organization called the "Arab Higher Committee." This organization was formed to oppose the immigration of Jews into Palestine and to oppose those in Britain who had begun to turn their support toward the Zionists. In that year the Arab revolts broke out all over Palestine and many Jews were killed along with Arabs who befriended the Jews. Then the Grand Mufti joined forces of Adolph Hitler in 1937 appealing to Hitler's own hatred of Jews and some claim that it was he who ultimately persuaded Hitler to begin the extermination of Jews in Europe in what we today call the Holocaust. If Hitler had succeeded the plan was to come to Palestine and kill all the Jews here. Finally, the "Arab Higher Committee" was declared a terrorist organization by Britain after they assassinated the British Inspector General of Palestine and slaughtered a large number of Arabs and Jews. The Grand Mufti was forced into exile in Syria then in 1941 he moved to Berlin where he worked closely with Adolph Hitler in the concentration and extermination of the Jews."

"How do you know all of this information?" asked Monica.

"Much of it is commonly known by the elders in Palestine. My father remembered it first hand," replied Dr. Abdul. "Muhammed Amin al-Huseini never returned to Palestine after his 1937 departure and he died in 1974 in exile from Palestine which by then had become known as Israel. During his life he was in strong opposition to our family, the Hashemite family of Jordan and in 1951 he arranged the assassination of King Abdullah of Jordan, my father's great uncle because he had given the title of Grand Mufti of Jerusalem to another person. After the death of Grand Mufti Muhammed Amin al-Huseini, his work and organization were taken over by his nephew Mohammed Abdel-Raouf Arafat As Qudwa al-Hussaeini whom you would better know as Yasser Arafat. To this day Yasser Arafat still refers to his uncle as "our hero al-Huseini."

"Wow, I don't know what to say," replied Monica. "In America all we ever hear about is what a great man Arafat is. Someone seems to have the information turned upside down. I still don't understand why you stay here. Al Zahra told me that it is because you believe that we are at the time of the arrival of Mahdi whom you believe is one and the same as the Jewish messiah Moshiach ben David. Is that correct and if so, why do you believe that?"

"Well the identity of Mahdi as one and the same as Moshiach ben David is one possibility that some of my close friends who are clerics believe. But they cannot express this publicly," replied Dr. Abdul. "Yet there is another possibility that they have considered."

"What is that?" asked Monica.

Dr. Abdul looked at Al Zahra for a moment then he looked back at Monica. "Well this is going to come as a little bit of a surprise to you but there are some clerics who believe that the Muslim messiah Mahdi is actually female. In Judaism, the Jewish Messiah must be male because he is a patrilineal descendant of King David. This does not mean that women are inferior. What it means is that this is simply the test that was given to the Jews to identify their messiah. Most Muslim clerics believe that Mahdi is also male but many also believe that he might be a she," laughed Dr. Abdul.

Monica shook her head and said, "Wait a minute, you are saying that the Muslim messiah could be female? I have never heard that." She looked at Al Zahra who smiled as she looked at Monica. "You didn't tell me that Al Zahra."

"I thought that my Dad could explain it better than I could," she replied.

"You see, in the line of descendants, King David had sons to pass on his seed. However, Mohammad did not. He only had daughters and all descendants of Mohammad, such as our family descend from his daughter Al Zahra, after whom this Al Zahra was named. So even according to our accepted line of descent there was a woman. This means that the Muslim messiah Mahdi could be female if the messiah will be descended from Mohammad as many believe. It could be that she won't be descended from Mohammad at all but will be from a Muslim nation where everyone born is automatically considered Muslim by the government."

"This is fascinating," said Monica as she looked at Al Zahra who laughed.

"It gets better," said Al Zahra. "Go on Daddy."

Dr. Abdul continued, "Now remember, this is only a theory, but there are some clerics who believe that Moshiach ben David, the Jewish Messiah, who is male, is actually the resurrected King David. At some point in his resurrected life he meets the resurrected Bathsheba, his beloved wife of three thousand years earlier, who is descended from Mohammed or who will come from a Muslim nation. He will carefully awaken her to her identity but he will remain locked in chains until she comes to a full awareness of first her own identity and when she finally understands, she will eventually obtain the courage to release him from his chains. But she must accept her anointing and will build an empire that will expand throughout all the Middle East. The people will love her and will plead to come into the empire she will build."

"This is fascinating," said Monica. "Okay, so how will the fanatical clerics ever accept that a woman might be Mahdi?

"They say that there will arise a woman who will have such power that even the most powerful spiritual leaders in all Islam will recognize her and will lower their heads to her. That will be the beginning of the acceptance of who she is. When this happens we know that the world has reached the appointed time. So, according to this theory we should be watching for something of this nature to occur and then we might well have found Mahdi," said Dr. Abdul. "Now, it is important to remember Monica, this is only a theory and it is considered heresy by many clerics. We won't really know what will happen until it happens."

"But how do we know that we are at the time of Moshiach or Mahdi or whatever?" asked Monica.

"There are many reasons," replied Dr. Abdul. "But let me give you one important clue. Al Zahra told me that she told you about the Jewish person they call "the prophet."

"Yes, she said that some believe he is Moshiach ben David."

"What I am going to tell you is something that he has revealed to certain rabbis in Israel who told it to me."

"The book of Daniel is a book of the Jewish Tanakh that was written over 2500 years ago while the Jews were in exile in Babylon. It is the same book in the Old Testament of your bible. There are two verses in the 12th Chapter that are very important for understanding where we are in world history.

Dr. Abdul continued, "In verse 12:11 we are told that from the time the daily sacrifices are taken away or prohibited until the appalling abomination that causes desolation occurs is one thousand, two hundred and ninety (1290) days. Verse 12:12 tells us that the one who waits and reaches the days of one thousand, three hundred and thirty five (1335) is blessed or fortunate."

"Now this is what 'the prophet' has revealed:

The Jews do not perform daily sacrifices since the temple does not exist in Jerusalem. So the term daily sacrifices, refers to daily prayers. On January 20, 1942 the Wannssee Convention was held in Germany. It was at that convention that a decision was made to concentrate and exterminate all Jews. This actually went into effect, and was first announced publicly by Hitler on January 24, 1942. Thus, on that date it officially became illegal to be a Jew in the nations under Hitler's control. This means that, figuratively, the daily sacrifices were abolished or more specifically, the daily prayers of Jews were prohibited."

"August 6, 1945 exactly 1290 days later, to the day, the US dropped the atomic bomb on Hiroshima. This was the 'appalling abomination that causes desolation.'"

"September 20, 1945, 1335 days to the day after day that Hitler officially began the concentration and extermination of the Jews, was the day of the final and unconditional surrender of Germany to the allies."

"Do you follow?" asked Dr. Abdul. "Let's establish a timeline."

"There was the announcement on January 24, 1942. On our timeline this is day one."

"Day One:

"On January 24, 1942 the daily sacrifices were abolished. On this day it officially became unlawful to exercise the faith of Judaism in the nations of Europe under the Hitler umbrella of influence. It was illegal to say the daily prayers."

"Day 1290

On August 6, 1945 there was the abomination that causes desolation. On this date the bomb was dropped on Hiroshima causing the loss of life of 140,000 people."

"Day 1335 September 20, 1945 was the day of the execution of the treaty between Russia, the US, England and Germany which resulted in the unconditional surrender of Germany."

Monica was silent for a moment then said, "This is incredible. I can't wait to tell this to my father."

"Now in the next verse, Daniel 12:13 Daniel was told to rest until the end then arise to receive his lot at the end of the days. This is a reference to the resurrection."

"You see," continued Dr. Abdul, "the resurrection appears to occur shortly after the event that concludes with the unconditional surrender of Germany. That occurred slightly over 60 years ago. If this is correct, then we are now at the time of the resurrection. Anyone alive today born after 1945, such as the prophet, could easily be a member of the first of those of the resurrection."

Monica looked at Al Zahra, then Fadilah and then Dr. Abdul. Each returned her startled expression with a smile.

VIII

While Monica and Al Zahra were visiting Al Zahra's family in Gaza, Aaron traveled to Jerusalem to visit his friend from Washington University, Rabbi Joseph Jacobson. As he arrived at the airport in Jerusalem Aaron was greeted by Rabbi Jacobson and his wife Esther. "Welcome to the Holy Land," said Rabbi Jacobson.

"Thank you Rabbi," replied Aaron. "I haven't been here in nearly 25 years."

"Please call me Joe," said Rabbi Jacobson. "The car is in the parking structure right out front. Did you have a nice flight?"

"It was long but the anticipation of arriving in Israel made it exciting," said Aaron.

As they drove through the streets of Jerusalem Aaron looked through the open windows in wonder at the ancient sites. The sites and sounds of the busy city were fascinating. The warm afternoon air combined with the aroma of the early evening meals cooking in many of the homes made Aaron anxious to arrive at the Rabbi's home.

"Here we are," said Esther as they drove up the drive to the modest but clean home.

"You have a very lovely house," said Aaron as they walked into the house.

"Oh, thank you,' said Rabbi Jacobson. "It serves our needs well. You must be tired from the long flight. You may use the room at the end of the hall," he said motioning down the hallway then leading the way.

"Thank you," said Aaron.

As Aaron followed Rabbi Jacobson down the long hallway to the room at the end, he noticed the arch of the ceiling and door frames of each room he passed. "How long have you lived here?" asked Aaron.

"I was raised in this house," replied the Rabbi. "I remained here until I left to go to the United States for graduate studies. My grandfather came here in the early 20th century and bought this house. It has remained in the family since that time."

"It is a beautiful structure. Do you know when it was built?" asked Aaron.

"We don't know for sure," replied Rabbi Joseph. "This part of the city is believed to have been constructed approximately 600 years ago. We believe the house was built about 400 years ago."

Rabbi Jacobson opened the door to the bedroom and Aaron could smell the fresh air from the open window as the curtains flowed gently in the breeze. Aaron placed his traveling bag on the floor next to the bed and walked over to the window to gaze upon the city below. From his vantage he could look down upon the Temple Mount where the Dome of the Rock shined in the afternoon setting sun.

That evening after dinner, they decided to relax in the sitting room at the front of the house. Rabbi Jacobson leaned back in his chair looking out the living room window onto the street almost as if waiting for Aaron to speak. Esther poured green tea into their cups.

Breaking the silence Aaron asked, "Did you know my father?"

"Yes, I did," replied the rabbi almost as certain as if rehearsed.

"Why did he take us to Israel that year?" asked Aaron? "If we hadn't gone to Israel my family would still be alive. How could that have been a proper decision?"

"You are trying to understand what is in the mind of HaShem," replied Rabbi Jacobson. "Let me tell you a story. It is actually a true story," continued the rabbi. "There was a young man in yeshiva studying to become a rabbi. He studied six days per week from sun up to well beyond sundown. He allowed himself one vice which was to play the Israel lottery. Every day for five years he chose the same number. He never changed it. One day he decided that just for once he would use a different number than the one he always selected so he chose a totally new number. On the day of the drawing he was not surprised to see that he did not win but much to his astonishment the number he had chosen everyday for five years was the winning number."

The rabbi paused for a moment as he gazed out the window and took a sip of his jasmine green tea. He continued, "The young Torah student was so upset that he flew all the way to Crown Heights in Brooklyn to speak to the Rebbe. He asked the Rebbe, 'Why would HaShem do something like this to me? Why didn't I win when I played the same number everyday and on the one day that I played a different number, the number I always chose won? The guy who won must have been a very righteous person.'"

The rabbi sat his tea cup on the table next to the chair, stood to his feet, walked over to the window and looked down upon the city of Jerusalem.

"What did the Rebbe say to the young man?" asked Aaron.

Rabbi Jacobson stepped back from the window and turned toward Aaron with a smile, "What do you think the Rebbe said to him?"

Aaron replied, "I don't know. He probably told the man it was HaShem's will."

"Actually, that is close," replied Rabbi Jacobson. "When the young man asked that question the Rebbe chuckled and replied, 'Nobody won the lottery. The person who had the winning ticket is the person who was chosen by HaShem to receive it. But while he received the lottery proceeds, you received a much greater treasure.'"

"'What did I receive?'" asked the young yeshiva student with a perplexed demeanor."

"'You received the knowledge that HaShem chose the other man to win. That is a treasure worth far more than the lottery proceeds. You received a firsthand demonstration of HaShem's power and it was intended just for you.'"

"That is an amazing story," said Aaron. "One can really see the divine in that story."

The two men sat in silence for several minutes. Aaron ran his index finger around the handle of the tea cup while Rabbi Jacobson rocked slowly back and forth in his chair that was not actually designed as a rocker but which he had pushed back onto its rear legs. Esther went back into the kitchen to visit with a neighbor friend who had stopped by to return a dish she had borrowed. Rabbi Jacobson looked at Aaron and chuckled.

"Aaron, would you like to see something amazing?" he asked.

"Yes I would," replied Aaron anxiously.

"Follow me," said the rabbi.

Rabbi Jacobson led Aaron down a long hallway to the rear of the home. They unlocked and opened a heavy wooden door, passed through, then walked down a flight of stone stairs into an underground enclosure. After going through another door leading out of the enclosure they entered a long tunnel which led to a large room. The large room had a table, several chairs, a desk, a glass cabinet which contained a Torah scroll, and a wooden bench. In the far end of the large room was a fireplace. Rabbi Jacobson went to the fireplace and moved a stone from its place just below the mantel. He reached in and pulled out a deerskin bag which contained a parchment.

"What is this place," asked Aaron.

"It was with the house when we bought it. We suspect it was built in the first century and this house was built above it to connect and conceal it about 400 years ago. There has probably always been a building of some sort here to conceal this entrance to the tunnels. This parchment has been kept behind this stone for as far back as anyone knows."

"What does the parchment show," asked Aaron inquisitively.

"At first we didn't know. It has lines that wind and crisscross. The only words in Hebrew letters are 'zeh po,' which of course is Hebrew for "it is here."

"What is here?" asked Aaron.

The rabbi laid the parchment out on the table and said, "Do you see all of these lines on the page? According to the story passed from my grandfather, which he received from the previous owner, it is a series of tunnels that run underground throughout Jerusalem. We believe it is a map of tunnels that were built thousands of years ago by the Jews to conceal something very important. Do you see the letter alef, the first letter of the Hebrew alphabet, here on the page?"

"Yes, I see it," replied Aaron.

"What we discovered is that the letter alef represents our present location here in this room which is the starting point, represented by the first letter of the alphabet."

"Have you found all of these tunnels?" asked Aaron.

"No," replied Rabbi Jacobson. "Many of these tunnels are blocked off with walls that have been constructed to block them and some were destroyed by cave-ins. We tried to cut through some of them but they are mortar walls 20 feet thick. Nonetheless, we were able to find a series of tunnels that lead to this location." The rabbi pointed to an "X" with the Hebrew words written above it, "Zeh po, it is here."

"What is here?" repeated Aaron. "What is this location?"

"When we got to the location shown on the map by following the tunnels at first we did not know where we were. It was just another large room like this one and there was a map, just like this one, except the words, "it is here," were circled. Using measuring devices and a tracking device we were finally able to determine the location of that room with the words marked on the map as "it is here." It is approximately 300 feet directly beneath the critical care unit of the Hadassah-Hebrew University Medical Center in Ein Kerem."

"I don't understand," said Aaron. "This map was made long before the Medical Center was built, correct? Was the map telling the location of the future Medical Center where it exists today?"

"We thought that was a possibility for a long time but then we noticed something interesting on the stone that covers the crevice where the parchment was hidden." The rabbi laid the stone on the table and turned it over to examine the side that always faced inward. Inscribed in Hebrew letters was the name, "Daniel" and the numbers "12:13." "If you look up Daniel 12:13 you will find the words from HaShem to Daniel that Daniel was to rest until the end of days then arise to receive his reward."

"What does it mean?" asked Aaron. "I always thought that verse was a reference to the resurrection of the Jews at the time of Moshiach. But what does it mean on this parchment."

"It does indeed appear to reference a resurrection but not Daniel's resurrection. He was buried in Babylon. It must be referring to something else."

"Is it saying that the resurrection will occur here? No, that can't be it," said Aaron. "The resurrection will occur all over the world. Is it saying this is where the resurrection will begin? Is it saying that the first resurrection at the time of Moshiach will occur at this location below or in Hadassah Hebrew Medical Center?" asked Aaron as he began to exhibit excitement.

Rabbi Jacobson laughed and said, "That is what I believe it is saying."

"Who wrote it?" asked Aaron.

"Well interestingly, the parchment in the room at the other end of the tunnels, which incidentally is 9 miles away, was written nearly two hundred years before this one according to the scientists who examined the parchments. The tradition from our predecessor home owners is that that the parchments have been copied over and over again in succession since the second century CE with only two in existence at any given time. When one starts to deteriorate they copy it onto a new one. The tradition is that these diagrams were written by Eliezar, the son of the famous Rabbi Simeon ben Yochai who authored the Zohar (Book of Splendor)."

"Kabbalah?" asked Aaron unable to conceal his amazement. "Are you saying that according to Eliezar, the son of the rabbi who first put Kaballah into a written form, the first resurrection in the time of Moshiach will occur at the location that is today the critical care unit of Hadassah-Hebrew University Medical Center?"

Rabbi Jacobson smiled, rolled up the parchment, placed it back into its deerskin bag and returned it to the crevice in the fireplace. He then replaced the stone. The rabbi turned and looked at Aaron as if to ask, "Any more questions?" Aaron did not ask any more questions as he stood looking at the stone that had been replaced to cover the crevice which hid the parchment.

Aaron drove the borrowed Jacobson Toyota into a parking structure near Rabin Square in downtown Tela Viv where he had agreed to meet Al Zahra and Monica. He found a space near the stairway on the third floor of the parking structure. Aaron exited the vehicle and walked swiftly down the stairs and onto the sidewalk. He turned and walked toward Rabin Square. As he approached Tela Viv City Hall he saw Al Zahra and Monica walking toward him and he began running. They ran toward him and he embraced both of them.

"It seems like I haven't seen either of you for decades," said Aaron.

Monica laughed, "It has only been a week Aaron. Are you getting sentimental in your young age? I think you just miss your 'hot babes'"

"I guess so," said Aaron. "I just missed you both."

"We missed you too," laughed Al Zahra. "Monica is just pretending to be tough."

They all three laughed and joked as walked toward City Hall.

"Why did you want to meet us here?" asked Al Zahra.

"I just thought it would be easier to meet in Tela Viv since that is closer to where you were traveling in the Gaza Strip and Rabin Square is a historical site I thought we could see."

"What exactly is Rabin Square?" asked Monica.

"Rabin Square, pronounced "Kikar Rabin" in Hebrew, used to be called 'Kings of Israel Square.' It was named Rabin Square after the assassination of Prime Minister Rabin in 1995. He was assassinated right over there at that memorial. Do you remember?"

"I do," said Al Zahra.

"Why was he assassinated?" asked Monica.

"He was assassinated because he signed the Olso Accords, which was a western effort to bring peace to Palestine and Israel," replied Aaron.

"Do you think the Oslo plan will work?" asked Al Zahra.

"No, I don't believe it will. Rabbi Jacobson and I were talking about that very topic a few days ago. Rabbi Jacobson said that Oslo was a noble effort but it is doomed to failure because it is based upon discrimination and separation rather than assimilation and tolerance as the Torah requires," said Aaron.

"I remember you told me about that when we first met Aaron. You told me that the Torah prohibits Jews from discriminating against other people in Israel as long as they observe the seven noahide laws," said Al Zahra. "Do you remember that we were asking if it is possible I am a noahide or even a Jew?"

"Yes, I remember," said Aaron with a laugh.

"Why are you laughing?" asked Al Zahra. "You don't believe it is possible anymore?"

"Oh no, that isn't it," said Aaron. "It just seems so far out of the thinking of traditional Judaism."

Monica began laughing as she asked, "What are you two talking about? Our little Islamic Al Zahra a Jew?"

"It is long and complicated," said Aaron. "The short version is that we were considering her ancestor Abraham and trying to see if it is possible a person is a Jew by observing the Jewish law without undergoing a conversion with a rabbi." Aaron paused and said, "Look here is the memorial where Rabin was killed."

"How was he killed?" asked Monica.

"He was shot by a Jewish orthodox extremist named Yigal Amir," said Al Zahra.

As Aaron, Al Zahra and Monica stood looking at the memorial Monica noticed the palm trees on Ibn Gabirol Street. "Hey I didn't know you had palm trees in Israel," said Monica.

"Wait a minute," said Aaron. "You are a Christian and your father is a minister. Did you forget the story about the 'triumphal entry' into Jerusalem? Now think, what were the people waiving when J'sus rode into town?"

"They were waiving palm branches," said Monica. "Oh duh," she laughed.

"And what do you Christians call that Sunday to commemorate the event?" asked Aaron.

"Palm Sunday," laughed Monica. "But how did you know all that? You are a Jew."

"I am a Jew but I am not illiterate," laughed Aaron as he put his right arm around Monica's neck and began rubbing her head with his knuckles as if she were a younger sister. Monica laughed, "Hey," she said. "Is there a method to your madness? You don't rub a woman's head like she is a little girl."

Al Zahra laughed and gave Aaron a slight shove on his shoulder. "You stop picking on Monica," she said.

Aaron, Monica and Al Zahra spent the day in Tela Viv. They had lunch and visited a number of historic sites and museums. That evening they went to Comfort 13, a popular industrial dance club in Florentin, South Tela Viv. They talked and danced until 2:00 am then took a cab to the hotel where Monica had made reservations. The three shared a room that night. Aaron slept on the couch while Monica and Al Zahra slept in the beds. The following morning they awoke to shining sun and a beautiful rainbow that had settled on the ground after a midnight rain in the land of northern Israel. Aaron thought about the prophecy of Ezekiel 37:22 concerning the nation of Israel. The prophecy was that Israel would become one nation and will not be divided kingdoms any more. Aaron thought to himself, "Sages have always believed this verse was a reference to the two kingdoms of

Israel in ancient times, Judah and Israel. Could this verse really be referring to the two kingdoms in modern times, Israel and Palestine?"

As they drove to the airport on June 23, 2003, Aaron asked Rabbi Jacobson, "Do you remember when we talked of the possibility that a Muslim could be a noahide, or possibly even a Jew?"

"Yes, I remember," replied Rabbi Jacobson. "As I recall the discussion was whether a person can convert to Judaism without undergoing a formal conversion process with a rabbi. In that context we discussed the question whether a noahide could become a Jew without guidance from a rabbi. We also discussed the prohibition on intermarriage with a non-Jew."

"If I remember correctly you said that the prohibition on intermarrying dates back to Avraham who instructed his servant not to marry a non-Jew and later Jews took an oath that they would not. You said the practice is discouraged by Orthodox Judaism and was expressly prohibited in the Talmud at Kiddushin 68b," said Aaron.

"Yes, today it is discouraged because of the diminishing number of Jews in the world due to assimilation and because of examples given in the Torah," said Rabbi Jacobson. "There are the practical reasons for not marrying a non-Jew and I don't know of any orthodox rabbis who would officiate over an intermarriage ceremony."

"If you were asked to perform a marriage between a Muslim and a Jew, what would you do?" asked Aaron.

"My immediate answer I suppose should be no, but it isn't that simple. The Torah tells us that those who marry non-Jews are lost to Judaism and we have found that through assimilation that is precisely what has happened. Before I could perform a marriage ceremony the non-Jew would have to convert to Judaism. The problem, of course, is that if someone is converting just to marry, then the conversion is for the wrong reason. We discourage conversion for the purpose of marriage and in fact we do not even assist in conversions for that purpose," said Rabbi Jacobson.

"What would you say if I told you that I wanted to marry a Muslim woman?" asked Aaron.

"That is a tough one," replied the rabbi. "I have a great deal of respect for you and for your judgment and I believe that any such decision on your part would be the result of great deliberation. I would be more than happy to help you work through this issue if you would like my assistance."

"I really could use your help with this issue. I am struggling," replied Aaron.

As Aaron walked through the gate, Rabbi Jacobson said, "I meant what I said. Don't hesitate to ask for help on the issue with which you are struggling."

"I appreciate that Joe," said Aaron as he waved good bye and walked to the gate leading to the airplane that would take him home to St. Louis.

IX

The next two years passed quickly. Monica, Al Zahra and Aaron grew even closer with time. They spent every day together when they weren't in classes. Al Zahra and Aaron had no further discussions of a romantic relationship after Al Zahra returned from Palestine at the beginning of the second year of medical school. Perhaps Monica created a diversion that provided a release from the stress of addressing the complications of an interfaith marriage. Though they did not discuss the possibility of a permanent relationship, they both thought of it with frequency and their love grew stronger by the day.

Aaron stood by the kitchen table in his aunt and uncle's home as he opened the letter from Hadassah-Hebrew Medical Center in Jerusalem. The letter read,

Dear Mr. Levy,

Thank you for your application to the residency program in the Department of Anesthesiology and Critical Care Medicine at Hadassah-Hebrew University Medical Center. As one of the world's leading teaching institutions we receive many applications from very highly qualified applicants to our residency programs which makes our decision a very difficult one.

I am pleased to inform you that, after very careful consideration, we have decided to extend an invitation for you to enter our residency program at

Hadassah-Hebrew University Medical Center in Ein-Karem, Jerusalem, Israel.

Please contact Marc Bloomberg to make arrangements for registration.

Welcome to Hadassah-Hebrew University Medical Center.

Very truly yours,

Aaron smiled as he folded the letter and placed it back in the envelope. "Sam, I just got an acceptance letter to the residency program at Hadassah in Ein Karem," he said carrying the letter in his left hand as he walked into the living room.

"That is wonderful news, Aaron," said Uncle Samuel. "I am happy for you but we are going to miss you."

"What is all the commotion?" asked Aunt Sarah who was just coming down the stairs.

"Aaron was accepted into Hadassah in Jerusalem," said Uncle Samuel.

"That's great, Aaron," said Aunt Sarah. "We will have to find a way to come and visit with you often. Hey Sam, maybe we should buy a small villa in Jerusalem. Aaron could save expenses by living there and we could come and visit. You always said you wanted to retire in Israel."

"Oh that would be awesome if you could do something like that," said Aaron. "Did I tell you that Al Zahra was accepted into the residency program at a hospital in Damascus, Syria? This means that we will be within driving distance of one another. She is still planning to return to Palestine after she finishes her residency. It appears we will be a short distance apart after our residency programs are finished."

"How is Al Zahra doing now, Aaron," asked Aunt Sarah. "We haven't seen her for several weeks. Is she well?"

"Yes, she is fine," said Aaron. "She is getting ready for final examinations. We will be graduating soon you know."

"Yes, it must be an exciting time for you, Aaron," said Uncle Samuel. "I remember when I graduated from law school. I felt like my life had not really started but had already come to an end. I had spent my whole life in school and I felt like my life was over. What was I supposed to do then?" laughed Uncle Samuel.

"I know," replied Aaron. "I have been having those same strange feelings. But it is also exciting."

Aaron, Monica and Al Zahara attended their graduation ceremony then made arrangements to go their respective institutions. Monica had been accepted into the residency program at the University of California, San Francisco. Both Monica and Al Zahra decided to fly home to visit their families before going to the place of their residency programs. Aaron decided to stay with his aunt and uncle until it was time to leave for Jerusalem. Aaron said "good bye" to Monica and Al Zahra as they walked toward security to board their planes. They shed tears and embraced each other. Each of them wondered if there was a possibility they would never see each other again. Two months later they were all in their residency programs. The Jacobsons had invited Aaron to stay with them during his residency and he accepted their offer. Al Zahra rented an apartment in Damascus where she did her residency and Monica leased an apartment in San Francisco where she did her residency.

In the winter of 2008 Monica was still at the University of California, School of Medicine in San Francisco. She had decided to obtain further training in obstetrics given that much of her work as a missionary would include prenatal care. Because she had expressed an interest in working in Palestine she received an invitation from Al-Quds hospital in Gaza City to spend December through March in the pediatrics unit. The University of California was very accommodating and allowed her to take the time off for her participation in the program. Monica accepted the invitation and arrived in early December.

Monica found the employees and doctors at the hospital to be very gracious and kind people. They tried to make her feel welcome not only in the work place but socially as well. When Christmas arrived the hospital employees went out of their way to make sure she felt at home and had the opportunity to celebrate Christmas. They put a Christmas tree in the hospital, had a Christmas party and exchanged gifts. Monica received a beautiful plaque from the hospital acknowledging her personal sacrifice in coming to Gaza during the Christmas holidays rather than spending the time with her family.

On January 3, 2009 Israel invaded Palestine. According to the reports Israel was responding to the continuous firing of Kassam rockets into Sderot and other areas near the border of Gaza Strip. The Palestinians responded in saying that the force used was excessive and disproportionate to the damage caused by the Kassams. As the invasion continued the number of injured Palestinians reached levels exceeding the ability of the hospitals to render necessary medical care. Monica saw numerous patients who suffered severe burns, most of them children given that she was in the pediatrics unit. She was told that the burns were caused by white phosphorus powder being used by Israel against the civilians. Monica found it difficult to believe that the Israelis would use such an extremely painful and damaging substance against Palestinian civilians. She heard that the Israelis were denying the use of the powder but there was no other plausible explanation for the chemical burns on the patients. The children would arrive at the hospital crying with their skin burned away revealing subcutaneous tissue and bleeding. She would attempt to treat the patients by anesthetics and sterilization of the wounds. Unfortunately, the hospital lacked the necessary anesthetics so there was little that could be done for the pain. The children had to endure painful showers and baths without receiving any medication for the pain.

In the evening of January 13, a large number of people were brought in to the hospital. The emergency room was in chaos. The hospital staff was treating the patients by triage. Only the patients who had serious injuries with a possibility of survival were receiving treatment. Those who did not have life threatening injuries or whose injuries were certain to be fatal received no treatment. Additionally, there was no pain medication to administer. As a result, many of the patients were screaming and crying making it impossible for the doctors and nurses to hear one another.

Monica was working in the pediatrics unit which had become an emergency room for children. She was especially taken by a five year old girl who was brought in with severe chemical burns. Her mother was screaming "white powder" over and over again. Based upon the information she had received Monica diagnosed white phosphorus. The young girl's face was red and raw and her eyes were bloodshot and covered with dried mucus. As Monica removed her clothing some of the substance came in contact with her arms causing severe burning pain. The little girl suddenly went into convulsions and Monica embraced her to comfort her causing the powder to contaminate her own clothes. As she tried to comfort the convulsing girl the child suddenly became limp and lifeless. Monica could see that the child had died in her arms. The little girl's mother became hysterical. Monica laid the girl on a bed and tried to comfort her mother to no avail. Monica continued to work frantically as the children were brought in but the death of the little girl in combination with the chaos was overwhelming and Monica broke down and began to cry. A doctor who saw what was happening decided that if Monica were to go out in the ambulance to look for survivors it would provide an opportunity for her to regain her frame of reference and composure. The doctor led Monica outside to an ambulance and placed her in the passenger side of the front seat and instructed her to look for injured persons.

In the early morning of the 14th of January Monica was riding in the ambulance to a district where the conflict was still raging. They had received a report of dozens of injured civilians in the southern part of Gaza City. As they drove down a busy street they noticed that people were running in the opposite direction from which they were traveling. "This doesn't look good," said the driver of the ambulance as he turned to avoid a truck that had broken down in the street. They pulled up to a crowd of people and Monica jumped out of the ambulance. As she ran over to the crowd she heard the sound of machine gun fire then she heard a deafening silence. She looked around and everything seemed like a dream. She shook her head trying to understand what was happening then she felt herself falling.

As Monica lay in the street looking up at the ambulance driver who was trying to lift her off the ground to help her to the ambulance, she suddenly realized that she had been shot. She also realized that her injury was serious. Although she could feel no pain she was able to place her hand completely inside of her own abdomen. She put her hand in front of her face and saw that it was covered with blood.

As the ambulance driver tried to place Monica into the ambulance there was a loud hissing sound from a rocket launcher then a blast and the ambulance exploded and burst into flames. Both Monica and the ambulance driver were killed instantly. For a moment everyone paused in horror at the site of the explosion of the ambulance then they resumed fighting.

On January 20, 2009, after 12 hours in the emergency room at the hospital Aaron received a telephone call from Al Zahra. He had been communicating on a routine basis with Al Zahra, who was working at the hospital in Damascus, so the call was not unusual though it was uncommon for her to call him at the hospital.

"Hello," said Aaron.

"Aaron, it is me, Al Zahra." Aaron could immediately tell that Al Zahra was upset.

"What's wrong Al Zahra?" asked Aaron. "You don't sound right."

"I have some really bad news Aaron," said Al Zahra. "Are you sitting? I think you should be sitting when you hear this? Are you sitting?" she repeated.

"I am okay" said Aaron. "What happened?"

"Aaron, I received a call from Monica's father this evening. It seems that Monica was working in Palestine during the recent Israeli/Palestinian conflict. She was in an ambulance that was hit by a shell from a rocket launcher."

"Yes, I remember that she was going to go to Palestine," said Aaron hoping that his interruption would provide a little extra time before hearing the anticipated tragic news. "Is Monica okay?" asked Aaron in a slightly panicked voice.

"Aaron that is what I am calling about. Monica did not survive. The ambulance was completely destroyed and she was killed," said Al Zahra as she began to cry again.

"A memorial service is in two days and will be held in her father's church in the United States. As you know, Muslims are not permitted to attend a service in a Christian church," said Al Zahra.

"Orthodox Jews are not supposed to either," said Aaron. "I don't know if we could even get there in time for the service if we were going to attend." Aaron felt like he was in a dream. "I can't believe this is real," he said. "Who fired the rocket launcher?"

"The Palestinians claim that the Israelis fired it but the Israelis claim the rocket was launched by Palestinians. We will probably never know. Aaron, why don't I come to Israel and we can be together while we go through this?" asked Al Zahra. "I am off work for the next four days. My father could arrange it for me."

"I think it would be good if we could do that," said Aaron. "If you make the arrangements I will pick you up at the airport. The only problem is that I am living with the Jacobsons. I am pretty sure they would not be comfortable if you were to stay at the house so we would need to get you a room. Are you okay with that?"

"Yes, it is fine," replied Al Zahra.

"Are you sure," asked Aaron.

"Yes, I am sure."

"Okay, then I will make arrangements to get off work as well," replied Aaron. "Just let me know when you will arrive and I will pick you up."

"I will be there as soon as I can," said Al Zahra. "I really wish I could hold you right now."

As Aaron hung up the phone he felt an overwhelming sadness. He went back into the hospital and explained the situation to the attending physician who said he would pass along the information. The doctor advised Aaron to go home and take the next few days off. That night, Aaron had difficulty sleeping. All he could think of was Monica and the day they first met. He wondered if perhaps he didn't love both Monica and Al Zahra equally well. He knew he had to get some sleep because he had to pick up Al Zahra early in the morning at the airport.

Eventually, Aaron forced himself to stop thinking about Monica and he finally fell asleep.

Al Zahra walked from the gate into the main part of the airport where she saw Aaron. She dropped her bag and ran to him. "Oh Aaron, I don't know how I am going to handle this. Monica was like a sister to me. This is really hard."

"I know," replied Aaron. "I loved her too."

Aaron helped Al Zahra with her bag. Neither one said anything all the way to the car. They walked arm in arm with Aaron pulling Al Zahra's bag which was on wheels.

"Did you tell the Jacobsons what happened?" asked Al Zahra.

"I did but they didn't know her, and they didn't know how close the three of us were, so they probably do not understand what a horrible loss this is for us. They invited us to dinner this evening."

"It would be nice to join them for dinner. Do they know I am Muslim?" asked Al Zahra.

"Yes, I told them. They are puzzled that we spend time together. Remember when you met my parents how open they were to you?"

"Yes, I remember."

"I doubt that the Jacobsons will be quite that open. This will be new to them," said Aaron.

"But I thought Rabbi Jacobson is the one who believed that Muslims could be noahides and possibly, in some instances, they could even be Jews." said Al Zahra.

"Yes, but it is one thing to talk about it in the abstract and quite another to put those beliefs into practice when it can mean that running afoul of the leading rabbis and even one's own congregation."

"I understand Aaron. It is one thing to talk about it but quite another to take a definite stand on an issue. I see the same thing in Islam," said Al Zahra.

"Do you think about Monica a lot?" asked Aaron.

"Yes, all the time," replied Al Zahra as her voice began to quake slightly. "I can't stop thinking about her."

"I keep thinking about all the fun we used to have together," said Aaron.

"Do you remember the first night we went out with her and we stayed at her apartment?" asked Al Zahra.

"Oh, how could I forget?" laughed Aaron. "I thought I had gotten involved with some pretty wild girls. You two would have made James Bond blush."

"We were just trying to be bad. We wanted to see what you would let us get away with. Neither of us was really like that," laughed Al Zahra. "We were both pretty innocent when you met us. And I am still am. Monica was too." As they walked, both Al Zahra and Aaron fought unsuccessfully to restrain their tears.

That night the Jacobsons were very kind to Al Zahra. They welcomed her into their home very graciously but their caution was apparent to Aaron if not to Al Zahra as well.

"Al Zahra, Aaron tells us that you are working at a hospital in Damascus. How do you like working there?" asked Esther.

"It is difficult but it also has its rewards," replied Al Zahra. "Sometimes working in the trauma unit leaves me emotionally and physically exhausted but I know I am helping people in need. It is that knowledge that keeps me going."

"Where are you planning to go after you finish your residency?" asked Rabbi Jacobson.

"I plan to work in a hospital in Gaza," said Al Zahra. "I want to be in a place where I can do the most good. Poverty is so severe in the Gaza Strip that people cannot afford adequate medical care. Most doctors try to get out of Gaza as quickly as they can. The people are left with the few who are willing to remain."

"What caused you to decide to become a doctor?" asked Rabbi Jacobson.

"My father is a doctor who works at a hospital in Israel. He crosses the border everyday to go to the hospital. When I was a child I would often go with him and study in his office."

"Which hospital?" asked Esther.

"The same one where I am doing my residency," replied Aaron, "Hadassah-Hebrew University Medical Center."

"What is his specialty?' asked Rabbi Jacobson.

"He is a neurosurgeon."

"Where did he go to Medical School," asked the rabbi.

"Egypt."

"And his residency?" asked Esther.

"Hadassah," she said.

"How do people in your country feel about your father practicing medicine in Israel?" asked Rabbi Jacobson.

"It is sometimes a little difficult," replied Al Zahra. "He also volunteers in Gaza on his off days so the people in Gaza are grateful to him. That causes them to tolerate his working in Israel."

"But he is Palestinian so why would he want to work in Israel?" asked Esther.

"My father does not hold any prejudices against people based upon their religion or ethnicity."

"Really?" asked Rabbi Jacobson inquisitively.

"Yes, he believes that Judaism is a divine religion and that Jews and Muslims are all descendants of Avraham."

"Yes, that is true," replied Rabbi Jacobson.

Aaron took a drink of his tea then said, "Joe, do you remember when we talked about the idea that a person could be a Jew even if he was not raised in Judaism and had never converted."

"Yes, I remember."

"And do you remember when I asked you if a person who observes the law of Moses and Rambam's Thirteen Principles of Faith could be a Jew without undergoing a formal conversion process?" asked Aaron.

"I remember that as well," replied the rabbi.

"Al Zahra and I have wondered if it is possible that she is in that category. Her family observes Jewish law and believes the Thirteen Principles of Faith though they consider themselves Muslim," said Aaron.

"That is an interesting question," said Rabbi Jacobson. "Your father has learned the law from his association with Jews in Israel?"

"Yes, that is correct," replied Al Zahra.

"Do you think Al Zahra could be a noahide?" asked Aaron.

"Oh, I believe that is true," replied Rabbi Jacobson. "Some scholars argue that this is not possible because Islam teaches that the Torah is corrupt."

"There are some Muslims who believe that," said Al Zahra, "but not all of them. In our family we believe that the Torah was given to Moses and that it is true and perfect."

"Isn't that a very unusual position for a Muslim?" asked Rabbi Jacobson.

"Yes," she replied then paused. "It is unusual but not unheard of."

"Do you think she might actually be a Jew?" asked Aaron.

"Well it is certainly an interesting thought," said Rabbi Jacobson. "I don't believe you will find much support for the idea within orthodoxy."

"But it is possible, right?" asked Aaron.

"I think it is possible," said the rabbi. "She is also of Hebrew descent. So even though she is Muslim, she most likely is descended from Avraham through her mother's female line."

"Her father's genealogy is through Mohammad and thus Ishmael." Aaron paused for a moment as if to ponder then asked, "Joe, what would you do if a Jewish person came to you and said he wanted to marry a Muslim?"

Esther looked at Al Zahra with a slightly startled expression as if she suddenly saw the light. Then she looked at Rabbi Jacobson.

Rabbi Jacobson, smiled and looked at Al Zahra who shifted nervously in her chair. She couldn't believe her ears. She glanced at Aaron in disbelief at what he had asked but she could only look at him for a second. She felt happy and frightened at the same time. "Surely Aaron is talking about us." she thought.

Rabbi Jacobson then said, "This almost seems like a continuation of the conversation we had several years ago when you were visiting me. I think I am now beginning to put the pieces of the puzzle together."

"I am just curious," said Aaron. "Al Zahra and I have talked about it a few times."

"Well as we discussed years ago, it would be a very controversial move. It would generate a tremendous amount of criticism for the rabbi who did this."

"If it weren't for that issue, would you perform such a marriage ceremony?" asked Aaron.

"Aaron, I think this might be an awkward conversation for Rabbi Joe," said Al Zahra.

"It's okay," said the rabbi. "I just realized why this has been such an issue for you. You two have been involved emotionally for a long time haven't you?"

"We have," said Aaron "but we considered this an impossible union."

"Well first of all," said Rabbi Jacobson, "if I were to agree to something like that there would be a long period of counseling so I could be assured it was the appropriate course of action. It is not something I could do without a great deal of deliberation and counseling and then I doubt that I could actually perform such a ceremony. It would be so much better if Al Zahra actually converted to Judaism but she cannot convert for the purpose of being with you. Her conversion must be real and for the right reasons."

"Joe, I would like to ask a personal favor of you. Would you be willing to consider this for us?" asked Aaron.

"I will." said Rabbi Jacobson, "but it is important that you not hold out hope for this possibility."

"Thanks," said Aaron. "That is all I am asking. We better get you to your hotel Al Zahra. It is getting let."

As they exited the humble home and walked to the car, Al Zahra said, "Aaron, I can't believe what I just heard. Are you saying that you would think about being married to me if Rabbi Jacobson would agree?"

Aaron laughed and said, "Why would that surprise you? We have hinted at this for years."

Al Zahra said, "In a weird sort of way, I feel like you just proposed to me. The proposal is somewhat conditional, but I think you are saying that if Rabbi Jacobson were to perform the marriage you would do it. Am I right?"

"Yes, you are right," said Aaron. Aaron put his arms around Al Zahra as they stood next to the car. They looked at each other closely for a few seconds then he kissed her on the cheek and helped her into the car. Aaron did not realize that when he took Al Zahra to the airport it would be the last time he would see Al

Zahra for over six years. After Al Zahra returned to Syria, the government began to question her visits to Israel particularly in light of her father's connections. Additionally, it was discovered that when she went to Israel she visited Aaron and that he was also a graduate of Washington University and a Jew. Aaron did not know that she had been questioned on these issues.

Nearly four months had passed since the death of Monica. After Al Zahra returned to Syria Aaron heard nothing further from her. Her cell number no longer worked and Aaron's letters went unanswered. Aaron was extremely perplexed and distraught. He could not understand why Al Zahra would suddenly stop communicating with him. "She must have met someone and he won't let her communicate with me anymore," thought Aaron. "First Monica and now Al Zahra," he said to himself. "This hurts as bad as when we broke up during law school," he thought. "Why does love have to be so painful?"

One day as Aaron was walking to the hospital he was approached by a young Arab woman who said, "This is for you." She placed an envelope in his right hand then quickly turned and walked away. Aaron looked at the envelope that had his name handwritten on the front as the addressee with no address. He immediately recognized Al Zahra's handwriting. He quickly tore the letter open and read a handwritten note from Al Zahra. The note said,

Dearest Aaron,

I hope this letter finds you well. I am so sorry that I have not been able to write to you. When I returned to Damascus I was told by the authorities that I had compromised the national security of Syria by coming to see you. I was told that I cannot contact you ever again. I have finished my residency and I am now in Gaza where I will work at a Al Quds hospital where Monica was working when she died.

I am so sorry that I couldn't contact you before. I was not permitted to call you or write to you. I found someone to take you this note. I have already been told not to contact you from Palestine.

I hope you can forgive me. I will always love you.

Your Beloved

Al Zahra

Flash Forward

As Katsín Akademái Bakhír (Senor Academic Officer) Aaron Levy drove the Humvee into the sandy ravine he heard the repeating sound of machine gun fire and the metallic ring of shots strafing the side of the vehicle. Suddenly, he heard a thunderous blast as the Humvee jolted upward and rightward responding to the impact of a close range Kassam rocket. As the vehicle flew through the air, in what seemed like an eternity, Aaron looked to his side and saw the body of Rav Samál Rishón (First Seargent) Jacobson thrown forward as his skull shattered against the windshield. "Michael" he shouted as blackness became his own limited awareness. Lapsing in and out of consciousness he crawled through the window of the overturned Humvee pulling his M4A1 assault rifle after him. Looking into the rear compartment he noted the lifeless body of Simon the nineteen year old from Tel Aviv, his body riddled with bullet wounds. The wheels of the Humvee continued to spin as he heard the familiar sound of angry Palestinian voices shouting something in Arabic concluding each utterance with "Allah." Instinctively, Aaron lifted the M4A1 above the bottom of the overturned Humvee and fired a round in the direction of the voice raising his head in time to see three Palestinian soldiers in black hoods fall to the ground, then he heard only silence.

After waiting a few moments to assure that there were no others with the attackers, Aaron began to examine the injured soldiers under his command. With a sense of responsibility and anguish he asked, "What's your status, David?"

David looked at Aaron with a distressed expression as he said, "I'm hit in the leg."

"You are going to make it," replied Aaron. "Hold on."

"Jonathan, are you hit?" Aaron asked.

"I'm good, but Simon and Michael didn't make it," replied Jonathan.

Grabbing the broken radio with his right hand to report his position, Aaron felt a cold shiver as he found the communication device inoperative. Reaching to his belt for his cellular telephone he felt a sense of relief as he heard the device power on only to find that he could not obtain a signal. "Do either of you have your cell phones?" he asked.

"I didn't bring mine," replied David.

"I don't have one," said Jonathan, as he began to look for one on the belt of Simon. "I can't find one on Simon," he said.

"Michael doesn't seem to have one either," said Aaron. "I am going to look over the hill to get our bearings. You fellows collect the weapons and supplies. We are deep inside Gaza. It may take us some time to get out of here. We are going to have to move at night so bring the night vision goggles. I will be back in a few minutes. If any more Palestinians show up, fight like you have never fought before. We don't want to be taken."

As he stood to his feet he felt a sharp sheering pain in his left leg and looking down he discovered a gaping wound at mid femur. He could not tell if it was from a bullet entry or a result of the crash of the Humvee. He did not recall feeling any pain in his leg earlier. As he ran with a weak limp toward the top of the hill, Aaron suddenly heard more shouting voices behind him. He cleared the top of the hill and dove to the other side. Lying prostrate Aaron looked back over the hill to see a dozen Palestinian soldiers run up to the overturned Humvee. His immediate reaction was to open fire then he realized that his gun was empty. He did not have time to reload. He watched in horror as the Palestinians began jumping up and down, shouting and firing multiple rounds into the Humvee and into his comrades who had not even attempted to return fire. "They must have thought they would be taken prisoner," thought Aaron. In shock at what he had just witnessed, Aaron could do nothing but lie prostrate in the sand daring not to move a muscle. As he watched, the image of the Palestinians shouting and firing guns into the Humvee reminded him of a time long ago which set him on the course of his military life in the Israeli Defense Forces.

As Aaron reflected on those earlier days he heard the voices getting closer. He raised his head slightly to peer over the berm and saw that the armed Palestinians were searching the sand for evidence of another soldier who may have been in the Humvee. Aaron began sliding quickly down the side of the berm away from the approaching militants. As soon as he was sure he was below the line of sight he jumped to his feet and began running in a slouched position down the hill as quickly as he could move. As he looked down at the desert terrain below he saw a cluster of buildings in what appeared to be a Palestinian settlement approximately 2000 meters in the distance. Approximately half way between Aaron and the settlement was a dirt road. Aaron's feet began to slide out from under him as he fell backward then began sliding down the steep sandy hillside. Soon his body became a human sled reaching a speed of nearly 30 miles per hour until his body became airborne for a distance of approximately ten feet before he landed hard on his back on the packed dirt of the roadway.

Aaron hit the ground with such force that his lungs instantaneously expelled their oxygen and he could not inhale for nearly a minute. Barely able to move without excruciating pain he rolled across the roadway, pushed himself off the embankment then began sliding face first down the sandy hill on the opposite side of the road from which he had fallen. As he slid down this portion of the embankment Aaron quickly reached a speed of nearly forty miles per hour. The ground felt like sand paper on his stomach and chest. As quickly as he reached the bottom of this embankment he was again thrown airborne only this time to crash through a wooden cover and splash into a muddy pool of thick liquid he immediately recognized as a cesspool of human waste. Aaron immediately knew that he had fallen into the waste disposal pond of the Palestinian settlement which was now only a short distance from him. Looking back up the hill he could see the Palestinian soldiers standing at the very top of the embankment looking far below. He remained completely motionless as he saw one of them point directly at the cesspool that had become his place of refuge.

The Palestinian soldiers stood at the top of the hill for approximately ten minutes has they talked and smoked their cigarettes then continued to look in the direction of the cesspool apparently suspicious that it could be a hiding place for an escaping Israeli. Not yet convinced that the sewage water was not the hiding place for an escapee, one of the Palestinians fired several shots into the water next to Aaron who remained motionless hoping they would turn away. Much to his horror Aaron could see that the soldiers were descending the embankment for a closer look so he decided to make a run for the settlement a short distance away. As he jumped from the pit and began scrambling up and out of the sandy edge of the cesspool Aaron heard a barrage of shots firing from the guns behind him.

He felt a sharp blow to the left side of his back causing him to lose his balance and stumble forward around the corner of a house made of stones and mortar.

As Aaron passed around the corner he saw a long alley leading through the center of the village for about a quarter of a mile. On either side of the street were houses connected one to the other made of mortar or mud and stone. Aaron began running down the alleyway. He could see people peering through the windows but they each jumped back as he approached hoping he would not see them. While he half staggered and half ran down the alley he heard the shouts of the Palestinians soldiers approaching the entrance to the alley behind him. As he ran past one of the houses the door suddenly opened and he felt a hand reach out and grab his right arm and pull him into the building. Whether due to weakness from the shot in the left side of his body or from a lack of concern, Aaron allowed himself to be pulled in through the door of the house and into a large room where he collapsed on the floor. The person who pulled him into the house ran back to the door and quickly pushed it closed. Aaron could hear the shouts of the soldiers outside as they ran down the alley looking for his whereabouts.

Aaron looked up from the floor of the house to see a large man who appeared to be in his fifties wearing traditional clothing of the Palestinians. "Let me help you," said the large man in English as he walked toward Aaron to help him to his feet.

"Who are you?" asked Aaron as he looked around the room and saw three younger men wearing blue jeans and pull over shirts.

"I am Jordan and these are my sons Sami, Sayed and Ahmed," said the man as he helped Aaron to his feet then over to a couch by the wall. "Who are you?" asked Sami.

"I am Aaron. Why are you helping me?" asked Aaron.

"We know you are an Israeli soldier and we know what they would do to you if they capture you. We would help any person in that situation," replied Sami.

Jordan opened Aaron's shirt to see the extent of his wound as Aaron lay back on the couch. "You have a serious bullet wound," he said. "We can't take care of it here. We are going to have to get you medical attention. Sami, go see if you can find Dr. Abbas. Don't say anything to anyone about Aaron being here. You don't know who you can trust."

"Okay," said Sami as he left through a rear exit of the house.

"Aaron, why don't you…" Aaron didn't hear the last few words by Jordan because he had lapsed into unconsciousness. As he lay on the couch Jordan pondered what he would do to get Aaron safely out of this Hamas controlled village.

After what seemed like weeks of sleep, Aaron awakened in a bed in what appeared to be a hospital room. His clothes had been removed and he had been bathed. He started to roll out of bed but felt a severe sharp pain in his left ribcage and left leg. Because of the dressing on the wound he could not determine the severity of the injury.

"How are you feeling Aaron?" asked a female voice. Aaron tried to turn to see the face of person who had spoken. The voice sounded amazingly familiar and caused emotions of happiness and sadness within a single sense of immediacy. Then she said, "Do you mind if I borrow your anatomy book?

Aaron strained to see who was approaching from the left side of his bed though he already knew. "Al Zahra?" he asked in disbelief half hoping yet half doubting that it could be her. As she approached from the shadow he could see the beautiful hair, facial features and striking figure of the woman he had come to love many years ago. "Is that you?"

The strikingly beautiful woman walked up to Aaron and placed her hand on his face. "Yes, my beautiful Aaron. It is me, Al Zahra."

Aaron felt overcome with emotion. He didn't know whether to try to jump out of bed to embrace Al Zahra or to remain under the spell of weakness that had been cast upon him by his injuries. "Where am I? How did I get here?" he asked.

Al Zahra sat on left side of the bed next to Aaron. "Aaron, you were shot while escaping an ambush by Palestinian militia. You ran down a hill to a village and found your way into the home of a Palestinian family who tried to help you. The elder of the home called a friend of my father, Dr. Abbas and told him that they were hiding an Israeli Army doctor named Aaron Levy. He called my father and asked what he should do. My father remembered the name and called me. In the meantime, during a house to house search you were found by Hamas and taken into captivity. They called the hospital and said they were bringing in an injured Israeli soldier who was going to be held prisoner in the basement of this hospital until he is strong enough to be transported to a prison. When you were brought in I was assigned to your care at my father's request. You have been here for two and a half weeks. Your injuries are very serious Aaron. We didn't believe you were going to make it."

"How long will I be here?" asked Aaron.

"They already want to transport you to the prison but I have told them it will be months before you will be healthy enough to live outside of the hospital. I told them that you are far more valuable to them alive than dead. They agreed."

"Who took off my clothes and gave me a bath?"

"I did," replied Al Zahra. "I must say you are even better looking than I expected."

At first Aaron was stunned at Al Zahra's comment then he suddenly burst into laughter which caused pain in his left side. Al Zahra laughed then became serious again and said, "Aaron, I thought I would never see you again. It has been over six years since we last talked." She leaned forward and gave him a gentle kiss on his forehead. "I have never stopped loving you Aaron," she whispered.

"Nor I you," replied Aaron as he closed his eyes and fell back into a slumber.

In the distance Aaron could hear the shouting of angry male voices speaking in Arabic which Aaron could not understand. He tried to clear his head to make sense of the events taking place before his eyes. Finally, he realized that he was awakening from a deep sleep. He opened his eyes and began to focus on objects in the hospital room in time to see a large man in a military uniform enter the room and strike Al Zahra with his hand on the left side of her face causing her to fall to the floor. The large man walked swiftly up to the left side of Aaron's hospital bed and lifted a rifle into the air preparing to hit Aaron with the butt of the gun at the location of the injury from the machine gun fire. As he thrust the butt of the rifle downward, Aaron felt a sharp pain in his left side as if someone had taken a sharp buck knife and stabbed it into his side. "Why would they engage in this kind of behavior?" thought Aaron to himself. "What accounts for this extreme aggression toward Al Zahra, one of their own pillars in the medical community?"

Aaron watched as Al Zahra slowly stood to her feet. Despite being viciously attacked by the soldier Al Zahra abruptly asserted herself with bravery that startled Aaron. She screamed something in Arabic at the large man that Aaron did not understand but which seemed to bring him into submission. She then grabbed him by the right shoulder and shoved him toward the door.

After Al Zahra had cleared the room of the Palestinian soldiers she walked over to Aaron. "That one was close," she said.

"What was that all about?" asked Aaron.

"They want to take you to prison," said Al Zahra. "I have had that same argument with them nearly every day since you arrived."

"Al Zahra, I can never thank you enough for what you have done for me. You have saved my life many times over."

"How could I have done anything else?" she replied.

"What are they planning to do with me?" asked Aaron.

"I really don't know," replied Al Zahra. "Some of them have said that they can trade you for Palestinians in prisons in Israel. That is why I always tell them that you are more valuable alive than dead."

"Israel has a policy against trading prisoners," said Aaron.

"I know," replied Al Zahra as she lowered her head and gazed at the floor. Her eyes began to water and the floor turned blurry. "I don't know how long I can keep them away from you. Some of them want to kill you."

"Oh that is no big deal," said Aaron trying to make humor of the situation. "We Jews are really good at dying. We have had more experience than anyone in the world."

"That isn't funny Aaron," replied Al Zahra. "My life after returning to Palestine has been like a horrible dream. Until you were brought into hospital I thought I should never have come back to Palestine after medical school. It is so hard here. Life seems so meaningless. And when I left from Israel the last time I saw you it hurt so much that I didn't want to live any longer. But now I know why G-d brought me back to Palestine. If I had not been here when you were brought in, there would have been no one to help you."

Aaron replied, "If you had not come back to Palestine you would not have interceded for me and by now I would be dead. You didn't know it but when you came back here after medical school, and undertook this tremendous personal sacrifice, you were coming back to save my life."

Aaron reached his left hand over to take Al Zahra's, left hand. "Thank you from the bottom of my heart," he said. Aaron and Al Zahra looked into each other's eyes for a moments then she leaned forward and rested her forehead against his forehead as the tears ran down her cheeks.

Aaron remained in the hospital in Gaza for four months. In time, a decision was made that he be allowed to remain in the hospital instead of being transported to the prison. This was attributable to the influence of Al Zahra's family. During this time Al Zahra and Aaron fell even more deeply in love than they were in medical school. Often they would sit for hours and talk or play chess. When Al Zahra finished her rounds she would always come straight to Aaron's room where she would stay with him until the early morning hours before she would go to her quarters.

Those closest to Al Zahra in the hospital would often ask about her strange relationship with Aaron. How did they know each other? How could she have such a close friend who was a Jew? Who is he? How does she know him? He is so handsome," they would say. "He has the most beautiful eyes of blue." Despite the never ending questions, Al Zahra was cautious not to tell anyone of her longtime friendship with Aaron from earlier days with the exception of one person. The only person to whom Al Zahra decided to share her most intimate secrets about Aaron was a nurse named "Farah." Farah had befriended Al Zahra when she first arrived at the hospital and she often went beyond the call of duty in assisting Al Zahra with the patients so that Al Zahra could spend a little extra time with Aaron. As a result of this closeness Al Zahra told her everything. She told Farah how they met in medical school, how Aaron had loaned her his anatomy book and how they grew to love each other in their forbidden relationship. Farah liked to hear the story so much that she would ask Al Zahra to tell it over and over again. She would listen intently and cry. Although Aaron often saw Farah in the hospital he did not ever know that she was the one who brought him the note from Al Zahra many years ago in Jerusalem.

One day Farah came into the room where Aaron was held prisoner when no one was around. She said, "Aaron, I think there is something you should know."

"What is that, Farah?" asked Aaron.

"You need to know how much Al Zahra really loves you. She would give her own life for you."

"I know," replied Aaron. "I love her too."

Farah continued, "Do you know how she puts her own life on the line to keep you from being taken to the prison or killed? She has been beaten by the security officers on numerous occasions and has been accused of collaborating with the Israelis. Sometimes they accuse her of being a spy. They also call her names like 'Jew lover.' I know there is nothing you can do but I just wanted you to be aware that she is your angel," said Farah.

As Farah stood up to walk out of the room she turned around and said softly, "Al Zahra is your angel."

Aaron nodded then rested his head on his pillow and looked at the ceiling. He was aware that she was doing everything she could to keep him from going to the prison or being killed but he was unaware that she was placing herself at such risk in so doing. He thought that perhaps he should attempt to escape so that she would not be in that position any longer. He knew that he could not successfully escape and that when captured he would be taken to the prison. But at least that way Al Zahra would not be in the difficult position of trying to help him. As he attempted to devise a plan to accomplish this it occurred to him that it could make things even worse for Al Zahra. She might be accused of knowing of his attempt in advance and possibly even be accused of assisting him. As he thought of what Al Zahra was going through for him Aaron felt a knot in the pit of his stomach. "How did we ever get like this?" he thought. "What happened to those wonderful days in medical school?"

Precisely how the IDF came to know the location of Aaron in the hospital in Gaza was never made clear to the Palestinians. On a summer morning at 2:30 a.m. two IDF helicopters landed on the roof of the hospital without warning. The soldiers jumped to the roof from the landing rail. They quickly kicked in a door on the roof and proceeded down the stairs to the basement area. A doctor opened the door of the stairwell to see the reason for the sounds. He pushed his head through the door, saw the soldiers then quickly shut the door. In the emergency room of the hospital an IDF Humvee suddenly crashed through the glass doors. Soldiers immediately jumped from the Humvee and began running toward the stairwell to the basement. By this time the Palestinian security forces had realized that the hospital was under attack. The information was played over the airwaves and the scene of the soldiers invading the hospital was immediately played on websites around the world.

As the soldiers reached the basement level of the hospital they opened the door of the stairwell to exit but were fired upon by automatic weapons. One of the soldiers spoke into his radio, "Security forces are in the basement area. We are under fire. We will take offense measures." Two of the Israeli soldiers returned fire with their M4 assault rifles and one kneeled to fire a rocket launcher into the area from which the fire was coming.

On the other side of the wall where the rocket launcher was aimed, Al Zahra and Aaron were running across the room toward the rear door leading to a rear exit of the hospital. "What if it is IDF?" asked Aaron. "Are we are running the wrong way?" He stopped and turned toward the sound of the attack. Al Zahra ran in front of Aaron pulling him with her hand. Suddenly, there was a loud blast and the concrete block wall exploded into hundreds of pieces. The blast knocked Aaron and Al Zahra to the floor. During the blast Al Zahra was struck in the head by a large piece of cement from the wall. She fell to the floor and was immediately rendered unconscious. Aaron pulled himself into a sitting position on the floor in time to see a number of IDF soldiers enter the room. As he waived the dust from his eyes one of them said, "Aaron Levy? We are here to get you out. Let's go. We don't have much time."

Aaron looked around the room to see if he could find Al Zahra. He saw her lying face down on the floor motionless and covered by a pile of concrete rubble and dust. Quickly he crawled to her to ascertain the extent of her injuries.

"Is that the doctor who kept you alive in here," asked one of soldiers.

"Yes, her name is Al Zahra," said Aaron. "We need to take her with us."

"We were told to extract only you," replied the soldier. "We have to go now."

"I can't leave her," said Aaron.

"Okay, we need to hurry then," replied the soldier as he got down on his knees to help remove the concrete and dust from Al Zahra's motionless body. Together they moved a large piece of concrete from her midsection and legs. “I’m sorry, but I don’t think she is going to make it Dr. Levy. She must have been hit in the head with one of these pieces of concrete then she was crushed by a larger piece. We heard the story of how she kept you alive and that you knew each other in medical school.”

Aaron and the soldier lifted her and placed her on a stretcher that had been brought in by another soldier. Al Zahra lay unconscious and motionless on the stretcher with blood pouring from and huge gash in the top of her head from which Aaron could see a portion of her brain protruding. As they began to carry her to the hallway they heard shots fired in the corridor ahead. Several members of the team ran out to meet the fire and quickly overcame the Palestinian security team then led Aaron out to the door to the roof. One of the soldiers took the stretcher from Aaron and he and the other soldier carried Al Zahra on the stretcher. The team ran out the door to the roof and the helicopter which was preparing to take off. They placed Al Zahra on the stretcher inside the helicopter then pulled Aaron into the helicopter as it lifted from the roof.

As the helicopter flew away from the roof of the hospital numerous shots were fired from the ground. Although some of the shots struck the frame of the helicopter none struck anyone within the helicopter. As they flew through the air across the border toward Jerusalem, the medic whispered to Aaron that Al Zahra was fighting for her life. Aaron could barely believe what had happened. He broke away from the soldiers who were restraining him and pulled himself up to Al Zahra’s side as she lay on the stretcher on the floor of the helicopter with her face covered in blood. Aaron put his right hand on the left side of her face and turned her head toward him. Her eyes remained closed. Aaron checked her pulse and noticed that it had stopped. He got up on his knees and began performing CPR while the medic adjusted the heart monitor to follow her heart rhythm. Her heart restarted but her pulse was very weak.

Al Zahra's pulse stopped again and Aaron immediately resumed CPR frantically as if Al Zahra's survival were dependent upon the degree of panic he exhibited. Her pulse resumed but seemed to grow faint by the second.

"Al Zahra, you have to hold on," Aaron whispered in her ear. One of the soldiers put his right arm around Aaron's shoulder and said, "Trust HaShem." Aaron turned to his left quickly to see who had said this. To his shock no one was there. "I am really losing it," thought Aaron to himself.

As they landed upon the roof of Hadassah-Hebrew University Medical Center in Ein-Karem, Jerusalem, Aaron noticed a crowd of people beginning to gather at the hospital. "There must be dozens of people down there and I see news cameras" said Aaron. "What is going on?"

"Those are the people who have come out to support you and Al Zahra" said a soldier. "The rescue efforts have been in the news."

"I don't get it," said Aaron. "How do they know about Al Zahra?" he asked.

"Dr. Levy, about a week ago the story of you and Al Zahra was leaked to the press. We already knew about both you and Al Zahra through our joint intelligence operations with the United States 10 years ago. About two weeks ago a rabbi in a temple in Sefed said that he had been contacted by a Palestinian nurse named "Farah" who told him a story about a Palestinian woman who is a doctor in Palestine who was risking her own life to save the life of a young Jewish doctor whom she had met in medical school in the United States and who was being held prisoner. She also told him where you were being held. Someone in the temple told a news reporter and within a week the story had hit the major news media all around the world. A few days ago it was decided that it would only be a matter of time before the Palestinians put two and two together and figured out that it was Al Zahra and you who were being celebrated all over the media. For that reason we decided to make a rescue attempt."

The following morning Aaron could hardly believe his eyes as he looked down upon the streets from the window of the Intensive care of Hadassah-Hebrew University Medical Center. As far as he could see the streets were filled with Israelis many carrying signs that said, "We love you Al Zahra." Other signs said, "Thank you Al Zahra." And some said, "Long Live Al Zahra." There were news cameras everywhere.

"The whole world is watching Aaron," said Dr. Schwartz who had been assigned to Al Zahra's care. "The amazing thing is that she is a Palestinian and you are a Jew and everyone knows the depth of your relationship but that you never got together romantically because of your different faiths. It is like a real life love story. The whole world is following every event minute by minute. The story is even on CNN and NBC. Everyone all over the world is praying for Al Zahra. They are holding rallies and prayer vigils everywhere."

Al Zahra had been in the hospital for two days now. The rescue had been performed on Shabbat since it would be least expected on that day. It was Sunday evening August 16, 2015. In every major city of the world people had gathered to show support for Al Zahra. The movement had gathered worldwide momentum and had become known as "The Prayer for Princess Al Zahra." It was covered on all the major networks. On CNN the announcer said, "It has been almost two days since the Palestinian doctor named Al Zahra Abdul was injured during an effort to rescue an Israeli soldier from his place of captivity in Palestine. The doctor caring for him in the hospital was his love whom he had met in medical school. They were never able to be together because he is a Jew and she is a Muslim. They once asked a rabbi in Jerusalem if he could perform a marriage for them. The rabbi never gave them an answer. His name is Rabbi Joseph Jacobson and we have been able to obtain an exclusive interview with him."

"Rabbi Jacobson, can you tell us about Al Zahra and Aaron," asked the commentator.

"Yes, it is a bitter sweet story," replied the rabbi. "They came to our home for dinner several years ago while they were doing their residencies. Al Zahra was doing her residency at a hospital in Damascus and Aaron was doing his residency at Hadassah hospital in Jerusalem. Aaron asked if I could perform a marriage between a Muslim and a Jew. The love between them was so apparent it radiated. It was a love of a depth that few people ever really experience. I can only describe it as a spiritual connection. I did not really answer them. Although an orthodox rabbi cannot perform such a ceremony, from that moment forward I have wrestled with this issue. It has been a source of tremendous turmoil for me. How can two people who are so obviously meant for each other not be together? They left our home and she went back to Damascus. They did not see each other or even have any communication for many years, then they were brought together again in Palestine under circumstances completely out of their control. It could only have been by the divine will of G-d. Now it appears that she will not survive. The doctors have given her family and Aaron no hope. They have said it is just a matter of time."

The news announcer said, "Rabbi, let me ask you a question. If you had a chance to perform a marriage ceremony for them now, would you do it?"

The tears began to swell up in his eyes as Rabbi Jacobson replied, "I don't know. It is all in our Creator's hands now."

XI

It was 9 pm at the Red Square in Moscow, Russia on August 16, 2015. Nearly 500,000 people had gathered to hold a prayer vigil for Al Zahra. They lit candles and were listening to a performance of "Jerusalem of Gold" which was Aaron and Al Zahra's favorite song when they were together in medical school. Near the corner of the stage an elderly rabbi from Lubavitch sat in a chair. It was said that he was 98 years old. As he sat he began speaking in Hebrew. Those near him turned to hear what he was saying but no one could understand him. He reached into a cloth bag and pulled out a large piece of a stone and gave it to a news correspondent who was standing near him. He whispered something to the correspondent. A news camera was turned to his direction and a microphone was placed to his lips. Then he stopped speaking and smiled. He looked directly into the camera and said in Hebrew, "I have prayed that I would live to see this day. My prayers are fulfilled. My good news is that she will live." Then the rabbi leaned back in his chair, looked into the camera then closed his eyes and breathed his last breath. Within minutes his words were translated into Russian and English. The video of the rabbi saying these words was played on news stations around the world. In nations everywhere people wondered "Was this rabbi giving a prophecy, or was he just expressing his dying wish? The doctors say she will not survive. How can this rabbi say something different?"

In Gaza at the hospital where the rescue had occurred, a large crowd of people had gathered also to pray for Al Zahra. At first the authorities told them to leave but as more and more people arrived they were allowed to assemble. In time the streets were filled with thousands of Palestinians many of them carrying signs in Arabic that said, "Princess Al Zahra we love you" and "Please Come Home Al Zahra." A Hamas security officer walked through the crowd wondering what had brought such a large group to celebrate a Palestinian woman who had protected and fallen in love with a Jew. "This is very strange," he thought but something enticed him to continue walking among the crowd also saying a silent prayer for Al Zahra. He was not alone. Many police officers and members of the security forces had begun joining the crowds in support of the nation's new "hero." As the Palestinian authorities began to consider the net effect of all the publicity they realized that this could be beneficial to the cause of Palestine. If the world made a hero of a Palestinian it would provide an opportunity to bring their case vis a vis Israel to the court of world opinion. Al Zahra would indeed be the first world hero from Palestine even though ultimately the image of Palestine could suffer from the abusive nature of the imprisonment of Aaron in the first place. Anticipating that the world would see the imprisonment of Aaron as a justified act, it seemed to be a minimal diminution in image the Palestinians might suffer if there were any diminution at all.

Throughout the Middle East millions of people had joined in the vigil for Al Zahra. It soon became known of her lineage to Mohammad the prophet and people began calling her "The Princess" or "Princess Al Zahra." In Damascus, Cario, Beruit and Bagdad people had gathered in large crowds to sing and show support for Al Zahra and pray that she would survive.

On NBC the news announcer said, "Yesterday she was a Palestinian doctor working in a hospital in Gaza. Today she is a patient in a hospital in Jerusalem called Hadassah-Hebrew University Medical Center fighting for her life. She loves a Jewish man named Aaron. Despite the depth of their love their faiths have kept them from enjoying the beauty of their romantic emotions. Al Zahra's doctors say this will probably be her last night. She is on life support and is not expected to survive until morning. Outside the door of her room in the Hadassah-Hebrew University Medical Center is a large crowd of family, friends and news reporters. Among her belongings at her parents' home in Gaza her family found a journal that they decided to share with the world. In her journal written approximately one year ago, after she had not seen Aaron for over five years, and long before they were reunited at the hospital, Al Zahra wrote these words:

'From the first day I laid my eyes on you Aaron I knew that you would have my heart forever. I knew that I would never love another they way I loved you. Those words proved to be so true my love. How I have wished that we lived in a different world where people didn't discriminate on the basis of ethnicity or religion. How I have wished that we lived in a world where a person's conduct and his kindness were valued more highly than the color of his skin or his ethnicity. In that kind of world you and I might have had a chance to be together.'

The announcer continued, "A few weeks ago while Aaron was in captivity, Al Zahra wrote in her journal again. This time she said, 'Today you are a prisoner in a hospital where I am your doctor. How I wish I could set you free. I would give my own life if I thought that it were possible to return you to your people in Israel. Someday perhaps the Palestinians and the Jews will be able to live amongst each other in peace and harmony. Perhaps someday there will be no hatred and strife between your people and my people. Perhaps in that day we can be together as lovers. Perhaps one day....'"

The announcer continued, "We will always have you in our hearts Al Zahra no matter what the future holds for you now."

In her hospital room Al Zahra remained in a coma on life support. Her skull had been surgically opened to relieve the pressure to her brain. Aaron sat next to her bed. Al Zahra's mother sat on the opposite side of the bed. Al Zahra's father looked out the window at the large crowd of people below. The rhythm of her heart remained steady but was growing weaker by the minute. They remained with her until the early hours of the morning. During this time, Aaron got to know her family. He had never met them before and they did not really know much about him until this story broke in the news media. Al Zahra had never told them about her relationship with Aaron for fear of how they might receive the information.

"It is too bad that we didn't get to know you years ago Aaron. Al Zahra did not tell us about you probably because she was afraid of how we might react," said Fadilah.

"I know," replied Aaron. "Once when we were in medical school Al Zahra said it would be so hard for us to continue our forbidden relationship. She said it would not be safe for me to visit Palestine."

Dr. Abdul said, "I always wondered why Al Zahra never showed an interest in men. Many men tried to court her but she always politely declined. To our knowledge she did not go out on even one date since returning to the Middle East from the United States. Now we know it was because she was still in love with you."

At precisely 2:32 am on Monday morning, the heart monitor alarm suddenly began to sound loudly and the indicator went into a flat line. A nurse immediately ran into the room and began pumping Al Zahra's chest as another nurse prepared the defibrillator paddles. A young doctor came into the room, took the paddles from the nurse and said "clear" as he placed the paddles to her chest. The charge caused no response. The nurse immediately began pumping Al Zahra's chest again until the doctor said "clear" a second time. The second charge caused the heart to start momentarily but after two erratic beats it stopped again. The doctors and nurses continued to try to restart Al Zahra's heart for nearly ten minutes but with no success. The young doctor pronounced Al Zahra dead at 2:46 am on August 17, 2015.

At 3:02 am Israel time a CNN announcer stopped delivering the news and looked at his monitor. He looked at a person off camera to his right to confirm that the information he had received was correct, then he looked back at the camera. He said, "It is with a saddened heart that I bring this information to you. Doctor Al Zahra Abdul is dead." He had to pause momentarily to fight back the tears then he continued, "It has just been confirmed. Dr. Al Zahra Abdul was pronounced dead at 2:46 am Israel time." The announcer stopped reading the text and said, "There were many of you who probably hoped that the words of the rabbi in Moscow were words of prophecy and that Al Zahra would survive. Even though I am not Jewish I was one of those who held on to this hope. It now appears that the words of the rabbi were simply an expression of his dying wish." The announcer paused as he looked down at his hands then said, "Al Zahra, if only the world had more people like you. We will never forget you. May you rest in peace and may those in your life in the next world be kinder to you than we were to you in this world."

At the hospital Aaron and Al Zahra's family asked the doctors if they could remain alone with Al Zahra until daylight. The doctors agreed and they left the room. For 20 minutes no one said anything then finally Aaron placed his right hand on Al Zahra's left cheek and said, "I love you Al Zahra." Al Zahra's mother burst into tears and her father embraced his wife to console her. They remained in the room with Al Zahra until 5:00 am.

When the sun came up on Monday morning August 17, 2015, the world seemed like a different place. Al Zahra, the new hero of Palestine was gone. Outside the home of Al Zahra's parents were flowers covering the entire lawn. People entered the lawn to place more flowers on the ground. Thousands of Palestinians had remained up all night holding a vigil at the home of Al Zahra's parents.

In cities all over the world people had remained up all night even after hearing of Al Zahra's death. Their hope that she might survive turned into tears as they huddled together until dawn. As the sun rose higher in the sky people in Israel and Palestine began their journey home. Around 5:00 am Dr. Schwartz came into Al Zahra's hospital room. He seemed surprisingly peaceful and calm. "Dr. Abdul," he said to Al Zahra's father. May I see you for a moment in the hall please?" As they left the hospital room Aaron looked through the door and noticed a large group of medical personnel, some news persons, cameramen and family members. A few minutes later Dr. Abdul came back into the room with Dr. Schwartz and a third man who was very handsome. The stranger looked surprisingly like Aaron with his light colored hair and blue eyes. He was wearing blue jeans and suede running shoes. He had on a loose fitting muslin pull over shirt with a draw string at the neck. In his left hand was a cloth bag Aaron recognized as a bag that holds a tallit (prayer shawl.)

In his right hand was a white robe which he placed at the foot of Al Zahra's bed.

"It is time to go now," said Dr. Schwartz. "Dr. Abdul has agreed to allow 'a friend' to say a prayer. We need to leave the room so he can be alone."

Al Zahra's mother looked at Aaron then at her husband and asked in a perplexed way, "What is going on."

"It is okay," said Al Zahra's father with a slight smile. "Let's go. We can wait in the hall. He is the one who is called 'the prophet.'"

Aaron thought, "This is very strange. This stranger who has entered the room is obviously Jewish. Why would Al Zahra's father who is Muslim allow him to say a prayer in the room with his deceased daughter?"

As they left the room Al Zahra's mother said, "I don't understand."

Aaron turned and looked back into the room. He heard the prophet saying a prayer as he pulled the tallit over his head. In the hallway there were approximately 200 people. Because of the international attention this matter had drawn, the other patients on the floor had been moved to a different location and news correspondents had been allowed into the hospital and in the hallway on the condition that they remain quiet. Aaron also saw hospital personnel and in the distance he saw his Uncle Samuel and Aunt Sarah who had come from St. Louis to be with Aaron. Aaron walked over to them and hugged them simultaneously.

"When did you get into Jerusalem?" asked Aaron.

"We got in last night," said Aunt Sarah. "How are you holding up, Aaron? We thought we would never see you again when you first disappeared. For a long time the government didn't know what happened to you. They just told us that you were missing in action."

"This is really hard," replied Aaron. "Al Zahra and I have been together every day for the past four months after not seeing each other for six years. It was like we never went our separate ways."

"I remember the time she came to have Thanksgiving with us," said Uncle Samuel. "I didn't know what was going to happen between the two of you but I never expected this."

"How is St. Louis?" asked Aaron.

"Oh, it is the same," replied Aunt Sarah. "Always delightful."

Aaron stood in the hallway talking to his aunt and uncle. Several news correspondents tried to speak to Aaron and Al Zahra's parents but the hospital security kept them away. After about a half hour a man in the crowd said, "Look someone is coming out."

The door to Al Zahra's room slowly opened and everyone expected to see the man who had entered the room to pray. As the door opened wider Aaron wondered why it was opening so slowly. Suddenly, he saw a female bare foot come through the opening in the door. A woman in the crowd screamed then fainted and a cameraman dropped his camera and began to run away from the door. Al Zahra's mother fell to her knees and began crying hysterically. Everyone began to step backward and some ran down the hall. Because of the sudden movement and hysteria of the crowd Aaron's view was now completely blocked and he could not see what was happening from his position. So he asked, "What is going on?" By now the area in front of the door of Al Zahra's room had been cleared and most of those in the hall had run away from the door of the room and some ran completely out of the hospital. A man shouted, "It is Al Zahra, she is alive."

As Aaron moved to the front of the crowd he saw beautiful Al Zahra come through the door. She was wearing the white robe that the prophet had brought into the room and placed at the foot of the bed. She had showered and her hair was neatly combed. In her left hand was a bag hanging by a strap. There was no sign that she had been injured at all. "Al Zahra," shouted Aaron as he walked cautiously toward her. "Be careful that can't really be Al Zahra" said a man from the crowd.

Al Zahra looked at Aaron and smiled while tilting her head inquisitively. "Aaron," she said in a longing way as she reached forward her hand to him. Aaron walked up to her cautiously then placed his arms around her. She embraced him in return. "Where is the man who was in the room?" asked Aaron. "What is happening?"

Hospital security officers ran behind Al Zahra and into the room looking for the man who had entered to pray. They looked out the locked windows at the ground far below and saw no sign of him either in the room or outside. A few moments later the security officers came out of the room and said, "The room is empty. There is no one in there."

Throughout the world on live broadcasts on every major network, people could see Al Zahra standing in the hallway of the hospital in front of the door of the room where a few hours earlier she had been pronounced dead. She looked radiant and strikingly beautiful in the white robe that the prophet had brought to her. Finally a news correspondent asked, "What happened to the man who was in the room, the one they call 'the prophet?'"

Al Zahra turned toward the man who asked the question. Looking directly into the camera beside him, which was broadcasting live all over the world, she said, "The prophet is gone for now but he wanted me to give you a message. He said 'Eternal life is not just a spiritual condition. It is a bodily event. The only thing separating human beings from this eternal life is alienation of man from fellow man. Before he died, our common ancestor Avraham took a stone of sapphire and broke it into two pieces. The stone represents the heart of Avraham. Avraham was a prophet and he knew that the descendants of his two sons would fight and kill each other for many generations and thousands of years. As a result Avraham's heart was broken so he broke the stone of sapphire to symbolize his broken heart that resulted from his foreknowledge of the fighting between his descendants. He gave each of his two sons, Isaac and Ishmael, a piece of the stone."

Al Zahra reached into the bag she was carrying and pulled out a stone. "Our family has passed this piece of stone down from generation to generation for thousands of years. According to our family tradition this is the piece of stone that Avraham gave to Ishmael, the ancestor to the Arab nations. It was passed down through Mohammad who passed it on to his daughter who passed it on to the present generation. It was given by my grandfather to my father. My father brought it with him from Gaza when he believed I was going to die. According to the prophet, the other half of the stone is possessed by the descendants of Isaac, the second son of Avraham. When the other piece of the stone is found and placed up against this part of the stone the two broken pieces will fit together perfectly forming the shape of a human heart. Then it will be time for the Arabs and the Jews to unite as brothers and sisters."

"This weekend of miracles was given to us so that we would know the truth in this story of Avraham. When these two peoples, the Arabs and the Jews, unite as brothers and sisters, and love one another in that capacity, then all the people of the world who accept this key of life as did our great ancestor Noah, will overcome illness and death. The key of life is represented by the two pieces of the stone which represents the heart. One piece of the stone represents love and the other piece of the stone represents forgiveness. This is the message that the prophet gave to me which I am now giving to you." Al Zahra held up the piece of stone so everyone could see it.

Toward the back of the crowd a man said, "I have a piece of stone. It is the stone that was given to me by the rabbi in Moscow who said I should give it to Aaron. I jumped on a plane and flew straight here all night. The rabbi told me that this was passed down from Avraham through his son Isaac, for this day. I didn't know what he was talking about."

The man walked forward with the stone and gave it to Aaron. Aaron looked at it and noticed its beautiful colors. He also noticed that it looked like the stone that Al Zahra was holding in her hand. Al Zahra looked at Aaron then held the piece of stone in her hand up towards Aaron. Aaron took the piece of stone he had been given and held it up to the stone Al Zahra was holding. Much to the amazement of everyone watching, the two broken pieces of stone fit together perfectly to form a single stone that had the shape of a human heart.

In Jerusalem, Rabbi Jacobson and his wife sat in their living room watching the live broadcast of events at the hospital. As he saw the two pieces of stone placed together the rabbi suddenly felt a sense of peace that he had never felt before. He stood up from his chair and looked at the television set for several minutes as the news commentators tried to understand and describe what had just happened. Then he turned and walked to the door that led to the tunnel. He entered through the door, went down the stairs and through the tunnel then walked to the door of the large hidden room. He passed through that door and closed it behind him then he went into the tunnel that led to the room nine miles away and 300 feet beneath Hadassah-Hebrew University Medical Center. The rabbi began to walk rapidly then as his excitement grew he began to run. He ran as quickly as he could through the nine miles of the tunnel. When he finally reached the room at the end of the tunnel, he ran over to the fireplace and removed the stone from the mantel. Out of breath and gasping for air, he took the deer skin cloth out of its cover and opened it revealing the map, drawn 2000 years ago, that showed the location where the first resurrection would occur in the critical care unit of Hadassah-Hebrew School of Medicine. The rabbi lifted the map from the table, held it to his chest, closed his eyes then whispered, "Elul 2, 5775. He is here." The date on the Gregorian calendar was August 17, 2015.